KRISTINE SCARROW

THE GAMER'S GUIDE TO GETTING THE GIRL

DUNDURN
TORONTO

Cover Image: istock.com/chuckchee
Printer: Webcom, a division of Marquis Book Printing Inc.

Library and Archives Canada Cataloguing in Publication

Title: The gamer's guide to getting the girl / Kristine Scarrow.
Names: Scarrow, Kristine, author.
Identifiers: Canadiana (print) 20189067764, Canadiana (ebook) 20189067772, ISBN 9781459744769 (softcover), ISBN 9781459744776 (PDF), ISBN 9781459744783 (EPUB)
Classification: LCC PS8637.C27 G36 2019 | DDC jC813/.6—dc23

1 2 3 4 5   23 22 21 20 19

We acknowledge the support of the **Canada Council for the Arts**, which last year invested $153 million to bring the arts to Canadians throughout the country, and the **Ontario Arts Council** for our publishing program. We also acknowledge the financial support of the **Government of Ontario**, through the **Ontario Book Publishing Tax Credit** and **Ontario Creates**, and the **Government of Canada**.

Nous remercions le **Conseil des arts du Canada** de son soutien. L'an dernier, le Conseil a investi 153 millions de dollars pour mettre de l'art dans la vie des Canadiennes et des Canadiens de tout le pays.

Care has been taken to trace the ownership of copyright material used in this book. The author and the publisher welcome any information enabling them to rectify any references or credits in subsequent editions.

— *J. Kirk Howard, President*

VISIT US AT

dundurn.com | @dundurnpress | dundurnpress | dundurnpress

Dundurn
3 Church Street, Suite 500
Toronto, Ontario, Canada
M5E 1M2

For all those who feel like misfits in the world:
Stay true to you — you are perfect as you are. You were
made for incredible things in this world. Believe it.

TIP LIST

- - - -

TIP #1	Be brave in difficult circumstances
TIP #2	Girls love a guy who's good with babies
TIP #3	Be a leader, not a follower
TIP #4	Stand up for what's right
TIP #5	Girls like a guy who's into their family
TIP #6	When she chooses you, you'll know
TIP #7	Doing the right thing isn't always easy
TIP #8	Things aren't always what they seem
TIP #9	Never underestimate your strength and abilities
TIP #10	Anger and jealousy are never the answer

TIP #11 Admit when you're wrong, apologize, and learn from your mistakes

TIP #12 Earn her trust

TIP #13 There's always a rainbow after every storm

TIP #14 Your true character is revealed when no one is watching

TIP #15 Even if the princess doesn't need to be rescued, she still likes a knight

TIP #16 Accept setbacks as another part of the journey

TIP #17 Tell her how you feel about her

TIP #18 Kiss her like you mean it

TIP #1

Geeky, pubescent boys aren't the only patrons at Gamer's Haven on this Saturday, and that is a rarity. The only females we usually see in the place are middle-aged moms looking for gifts for their sons at Christmastime or their birthdays. Otherwise, the clientele is all about the same. There isn't a dress code for the store, at least not one that we are aware of, but the standard gamer's outfit is usually the same: a comic-inspired T-shirt, loose-fitting jeans that have to be continually hiked up because gamers don't believe in belts apparently, and some Converse sneakers — well-worn and dirty. Most of us have shaggy hair that may or may not have been washed or combed, and we all look like we're chronically tired; if one were to take a poll to see how many customers had purchased *Monster Hunter: World* on its release day, the tired eyes would be explained.

It's Cooper who tips me off to the girl in the store. Because Gamer's Haven isn't known as the place to find girls, no one usually pays much attention to who comes in. I'm in the zone playing *Sea of Thieves* when Cooper starts elbowing me.

"Mess off, Coop. You'll get your turn." I shake him off with my hand in between plays.

"Your loss, Zach." Cooper turns on his heel and strides away. I whip my head around quickly to see what he's so excited about, and then I see her.

She's wearing a denim skirt, purple suede knee-high boots, a bright orange T-shirt, and a rainbow-coloured scarf around her neck. Her auburn hair is pulled into a high ponytail, and the bottom of it almost reaches the base of her spine. Her arms are bare and pale. I can't help but stare at her profile. I abandon the game and rush after Cooper, hoping to catch a better glimpse of the girl.

She's standing in front of the *Zelda* display. I could pretend that I'm buying it and make small talk with her. But what would I say? "Come here often?" "You like this game?" "Ever play this before?" All of it sounds lame. But I decide I have to rush in before Cooper does. I pick up my pace, but Cooper detours to the *Okami HD* display instead. He isn't trying to show me the girl? His eyes were on something else instead? Was he crazy?

I'm happy that he's distracted by something else, but now I have to try to play it cool and get closer without her thinking I'm a total stalker. I move one display over and turn my head as casually as I can. She's reading the back of a *Legend of Zelda: Breath of the Wild* case. Stray locks of her hair curl around her face. She's wearing soft makeup, and when she looks back up toward the display, I can see her bright green eyes. She's even more beautiful than I thought.

I have a stunning burst of courage and decide to act on it before I never see her again.

"Need any help?" I ask. She doesn't even look up at me.

"You work here?"

"Uh, no. But I happen to know a lot about video games. Like the one you're holding — it's been popular in the gaming world for a couple of years now." Maybe I can help with her decision-making.

"But is it as good as *Ocarina of Time* or *Twilight Princess*?"

I don't mean for my jaw to hang open, but it does.

"Because it seems to me that this interface is a lot less sophisticated than the one in *Twilight Princess*."

She finally looks up at me, just in time for me to close my mouth again.

"You're a gamer?" I ask.

"If that's what you want to call me," she responds. "Is that allowed? Or are you going to tell me it's a guy thing and I should move on to something a little more girly?" Her voice is bitter.

"No, not at all!" I say, putting my hands up in front of my chest like I'm being arrested. "I think that's awesome!"

She steps closer, her long ponytail swishing toward me, and I can smell her shampoo, a combination of honey and coconut. I want to drink it all in, her smell, her eyes, the fact that the goddess gamer of my dreams is standing in front of me.

"I'm not sure it's worth the money. Honestly, I think I'll wait for the next sequel."

She sets the plastic case down and turns to leave. I want to follow her, ask her more questions, and find out her name, but she turns so fast I just sputter nonsense to myself.

"Hi, I'm Zachary. It's so nice to meet you," I whisper, holding out my hand for the now-invisible girl to shake. "You know, if I were you, I'd wait for the sequel. Better interface." That could have gone so much better.

"Dude, you missed it," Cooper says over my shoulder. "Chris was unpacking the new shipment. *Dissidia Final Fantasy* is back in stock!"

"Yeah, and you just missed the girl of my dreams walking out of this store."

I can no longer see her bobbing ponytail. She's obviously exited the store and turned to the main mall corridor.

"Okay," Cooper says, rolling his eyes.

"Mall closes in five minutes, boys," the manager, Chris, calls out. I check my watch and, sure enough, it's closing time. We are the only two customers left in the store. "You guys buying anything or can I cash out?"

Neither of us has enough money; we like to come and play the demos when we're bored and broke. Chris never seems to mind since we tend to buy our games from him when we do have money. When today turned into a stormy day, there wasn't much else to do.

"Go for it," Cooper replies. He and I stand side-by-side, our hands stuffed in our pockets.

"Sounds like the storm is picking up speed," Chris tells us. "Was supposed to hit south of us but instead it's veered north. They've issued a tornado warning."

"Really?" I say nonchalantly. Summer in Saskatchewan often means high temperatures, and with them there are often severe thunderstorms and tornado warnings. Most of the time the storms are nothing to worry about. The wind typically picks up, we get thunder and lightning, maybe some hail rolls through, and then things settle down. Someone may spot a funnel cloud or two, which may or may not touch down. Often the tornadoes touch down on open prairie and no one gets hurt. At least that's how I think of the tornadoes we get.

"Sounds pretty bad," Chris continues. "I guess the high winds are causing a lot of damage already. A tornado touched down a couple of hours west. My wife called to say there's been some flooding in different areas of the city. Apparently, my basement is taking on water."

We both groan. That happened at my house once, and it wasn't fun. Dad and I waded around in our rubber boots in ankle-deep water trying to salvage what we could. You wouldn't think a couple of inches of water could do much, but it wrecked almost everything.

"Wanna go?" I ask. Cooper nods and we shuffle out of the store. The mall is practically deserted already. Cooper fishes for his car keys in the pocket of his hoodie.

And then the lights go out.

TIP #2

Girls love a guy who's good with babies

"What's going on?" Chris's voice rises. The entire mall is black, except for the lit exit sign pointing to one of the entrances. Since we're still in front of his store, we decide to go back in.

"I thought I had a flashlight around here somewhere." We can hear things spilling onto the ground as Chris fumbles in the dark.

"Well, this is a first," Cooper says. It sounds like he's smiling. We both pull out our phones.

"Need a light?" I ask Chris, using the flashlight on my iPhone.

"Yeah, that'll help."

The light from the iPhone is enough for him to discover that the flashlight he thought he had by the register is no longer there.

"Maybe it's in the back. You want to come and shine the light back there for me?"

The three of us shuffle toward the storage room at the rear of the store. Chris kicks a couple of boxes out of the way so that the three of us can fit.

"Careful. It's a little crowded in here," Chris warns.

Boxes are stacked almost to the ceiling with stock for the store. Metal racks line one wall, and random pieces of shelving that have broken off litter the floor. There's a small wooden desk against the wall, but the surface is so cluttered, it's hard to know what anything is.

"I'll check this drawer," Chris says, pointing to the right-hand side of the desk. I shine the light toward it.

"Bingo!" Chris says. It's a miracle he'd find anything in this room. He picks up a medium-sized black flashlight and flicks it on. It illuminates the room even more.

"Maybe you should make sure your safe is locked," Cooper says.

"Good thinking. Thanks. I guess I'm feeling a little flustered," Chris replies. "My wife is due to have a baby any time now. She called me earlier saying that she was starting to have contractions. It's all I can think about."

"Wow. That's cool. First one?" I ask.

"Yup. It's exciting, but I'm also scared out of my wits," Chris admits.

Cooper and I chuckle.

Chris examines the safe and makes sure it's locked. "Sure hope this power outage passes soon. Why don't you boys head out? Get home before this storm gets any worse. I'm good now that I have this flashlight. Now I just have to find where I put my phone." He starts rummaging through the papers on his desk.

"Yeah, I better get home," Cooper says. "It's my mom's birthday today and we're going out for supper."

"All right, see you later, Chris." I follow Cooper back out of the store.

"Thanks for your help!" Chris calls out after us.

The mall takes on a whole new atmosphere with the lights out. The metal security grates are already pulled across their store entrances. It feels more like walking through a dark prison than a shopping centre.

We pass the food court and see that it's deserted. All of the restaurants have closed up already. Only the red exit sign by the entrance glows. Outside the glass doors, it's dark and gloomy; the rain is coming down in sheets.

"It's weird. There's no one around. Did everyone go home already?"

"Nope. Everyone's over there." Cooper points. Sure enough, down the next corridor there's a group of about thirty people. As we approach, we see a security guard standing by the elevators.

"I'm sorry, but none of you can go through here," he says to the group.

"I need to get home," a man in a business suit grumbles.

"Me, too," echo a few others.

"We cannot grant access to this area at the moment," the guard repeats. He's over six feet tall and easily three hundred pounds. He stands on the balls of his feet in front of the elevators and the stairway, poised like an

Atari paddle playing *Pong*, ready to cover whatever area he needs to.

"But my car is down there!" the man in the suit says, his voice rising.

"I understand, sir, but you have to remain here until we can give the all-clear. With the power outage, we've encountered a situation."

"What kind of situation?" the man's voice booms. "I've got a Porsche Cayenne down there. If anything happens to it, this mall is going to pay." He tugs on his shirt collar, his face reddening.

Cooper whistles under his breath. "Way to announce that, buddy."

Two guys in their mid-twenties smile, and one of them rubs his hands together. They're both thin and wiry, with hair shaved into brush cuts, and facial hair carefully crafted into short goatees. They could easily be brothers. They're wearing full track suits, one in navy and one in black, and white running shoes. One is wearing a gold chain-link necklace that hangs over a white shirt.

"A Porsche, hey?" I hear one of them say. They lick their lips like Cheshire Cats.

"Better hope that guy makes it to his car before those two do," Cooper says, leaning into me. I laugh. He's seeing the same thing I am.

"What's the problem?" a woman calls out.

Others join in. "Yeah! What's going on?"

"It seems there's been a water main break of some sort outside. We have to make sure it's safe to exit." The security guard's ID tag hangs from a lanyard on his neck. His name is George.

"George," I say, hoping that using his first name will help, "you're saying we can exit through the other doors at least?"

"It might not be safe there either," George says.

"Safe?!" the man in the suit pipes in. "Why wouldn't it be safe?!"

"It's dark and there's water everywhere. We can't let anyone out at the moment, sir. I need you all to be patient while we figure this out."

A few people grumble. A woman starts pushing a stroller back and forth as the baby inside lets out a cry. A couple of middle-graders sprawl out on the floor and stare up at the ceiling.

"Liam, Henry — get up. The floor is dirty!" the woman beside them urges. They just laugh and stay put. I can't blame them. I want somewhere to sit, too. The only bench nearby is occupied by an elderly couple, which I'm glad to see.

I'm getting antsy standing here.

It's hard to make out the faces of most of the people waiting unless you're up close with them, but the darkness also makes it so that we can move around without everyone seeing us.

"Are you thinking what I'm thinking?" Cooper asks. I've been looking around for an alternate exit.

"Should we go back to the food court doors?" I whisper. "We can text our parents to come get us there."

"Yeah, but what about my car?" Cooper asks.

"I know, but you have to go. Your parents can bring you back to get the car later."

Coop starts texting his dad so I start texting my parents, too.

"Whoever answers first, that's who'll pick us up," Cooper decides.

My parents are at home as far as I know. Dad's finishing our basement so that I can have my own room down there. I'm excited about it — I'm looking forward to the privacy and some distance from my ten-year-old brother, Marshall, who follows me around more than our dog, Jasper, whenever I'm home.

"My dad's drywalling today," I remind Cooper.

"Sweet. Operation Zach's Lair almost complete ..."

My lair will be pretty lame next to Cooper's. His family has a lot of money and pretty much gives him whatever he wants. He has half of the basement in his parents' huge walkout estate. He has his own home theatre room complete with virtually every gaming system that's ever come out. The only restriction they put on him is that he's given an allowance for spending money and once it's gone, he has to wait until the following month. The difference is, he gets about triple what I get in a month. I often struggle to keep up with what he wants to do based on how much money I have.

I want to get a part-time job, but my parents don't really want me to. They're super focused on my grades and on my getting into whatever university program I want. I'm not clear yet on my path, but my grades are pretty good and chances are when the time comes, I'll be able to apply for medicine, dentistry — whatever I want. My dad is hoping I'll eventually go to med school. Certain things fascinate me about medicine, especially the finely tuned aspects of surgery, but I'm not sure I want to spend all the gruelling hours required to become a surgeon, not to mention do the work itself.

Cooper's parents are both lawyers, and they've been grooming him for law school since he was about four years old. I don't think he's ever contemplated anything else for his career. He doesn't have a job either; his parents are also hyper-focused on his grades. Luckily, school comes pretty easily to both of us.

_ _ Storm's getting bad. We'll pick you up. [6:15 p.m.]

It's Cooper's dad. Cooper texts back.

_ _ Zach is here too, can't get to my car, water main break. [6:16 p.m.]

_ _ We'll take him home. Reservations are for 7. Be ready. South doors. [6:16 p.m.]

"They're coming?"

"Yup. We gotta go down to the south doors."

We step back from the crowd and then turn quickly to shuffle past them and head for the south side of the mall. We go as fast as we can so George doesn't spot us, but no one seems to pay us any attention. George is too busy between talking on his radio and trying to calm the crowd around him.

We don't encounter anyone on our way. It's eerie to be in this darkened building and not see anyone.

"Oh my God, look at it outside …" I can't believe my eyes. The rain is coming down so hard that you can't even see the sidewalk ten feet away. The newer spindly trees planted around the perimeter of the mall are bent almost completely sideways from the wind. The busy road that surrounds the mall could be deserted for all we know because we can't see behind the curtain of grey that masks the world outside.

"That's insane!" Cooper says, wide-eyed.

"Wow," I whisper. I push on the door to step outside, but it's locked. "What?!" I push harder. It's sealed tight.

"Do you need some help?" Cooper teases. He lines up beside me and gives the door a good shove. It doesn't budge. "Are you kidding me? We're locked in?!"

It doesn't seem possible. We both stand there, stunned. Then Cooper points. "It looks like there's a stairwell here!" A big grey metal door marked "mall staff only" is tucked into a small corridor. "I'm taking the stairs." He flings open the door and starts down the stairs. I'm frozen on the spot. It says it's for staff only. I don't want to get in trouble.

"You coming or what?" Cooper calls up to me from the first landing just before the door swings shut.

If we can just get downstairs and get to the car, we can get out of here right away and none of our parents would need to come. He's right; it's the best option. I take a deep breath and follow him. Hopefully this staircase will lead to the underground parking lot.

We turn to go down the final flight and freeze in our tracks.

"Uh, I don't think we should go down there," I stammer. Water is rushing into the stairwell from underneath the metal door at the bottom. The water is rising and has already covered the bottom stair.

"What is going on?!" Cooper moves down closer. "Help me open this door."

"Is this a good idea?" I ask. "Maybe we should just go back and wait with the others."

"Okay, you sissy, and then maybe we'll be here all night. C'mon, I'm sure we'll get through here."

We have to step right into the water in order to pry open the door. I look down at my shoes and start to kick them off.

"Are you kidding me?" Cooper says, shaking his head.

"At least let me roll up my jeans then," I say. He laughs and waits for me to roll up my jeans. We step into the water. It's icy cold.

Right away the water feels like daggers on my feet and shins. "Could this water be any colder?"

"Will you just help me get this open?" Cooper says. He's tugging on the door without much success.

I grab the top part of the handle while he takes the bottom and we pull as hard as we can. It starts to give, a gush of water rushes in, and then the door sucks back to a closed position before we can get around it.

"On three," I say. We count and try again and more water rushes through. Now the second stair is covered and the water is up well past our ankles.

"Where is all of this water coming from?" I say.

We're both panting from pulling so hard.

"Once more?" Cooper asks and I nod.

This time, we pry the door open enough for Cooper to get his shoulder through before the door starts to pull closed again.

"Zach!" he cries out. I pull as hard as I can, my whole body bent back toward the stairs.

"I don't want you to get crushed!" I say, pulling. My heart is racing.

"I'm in. C'mon!" He slips around the door and digs his feet into the ground to push the door open with his back. Water continues to pour in.

I make it around the door just as Cooper loses his footing and the door slams shut behind us.

"Whew — that was close!" I pant. But nothing could have prepared me for what's next. The entire underground parking lot is flooded. Icy water laps at our kneecaps. It's about a foot high, and the tires of all the cars are half-submerged. There's no way anyone will be leaving in their car.

"Zach!" Cooper yells, pointing to the other side of the lot.

Cars are floating at the far end. Literally bouncing on the water and tapping into each other like bumper cars.

"This is not good," I say softly.

"We have to go back upstairs," Cooper says. "We can tell them what we've seen."

"A water main break can do all of this?" I wonder.

"Well, look, it's raining like crazy, too …"

It's been raining all day. It just seems so strange to me that cars are actually floating.

"I hope we can get that door open again." We use all of our might and the door comes open enough for both of us to shove our way through before it slams shut again.

We run up the stairs, splattering water everywhere. The rubber on our wet shoes makes loud, squeaky sounds and water squirts out of them like sponges being squeezed with every step.

The mall is still dark. Cooper's phone dings with a text.

– – We can't get there. The bridge has been washed out!
   We'll try going around the city. [6:45 p.m.]

Coop shows me his phone as he types.

– – What?? [6:45 p.m.]

– – There's flooding. It washed out the bridge. [6:46 p.m.]

It doesn't seem possible. I mean, we knew there were going to be thunderstorms today, but no one expected flooding. Gateway Bridge is the main access point to this mall since it's one of the first buildings in a new commercial development. There's a grid road nearby that takes you out to one of the main highways, but it'll take a lot of time to get around the city and link up to it.

"So, now what? We're stuck?!" The two of us just stare at each other.

"Stuck in the mall?" Cooper says. "I suppose there are worse things."

"Well, it'd be better with lights on," I say. "Might as well go back to the group."

We trudge back to the group. By now, many people are sitting on the ground. Some are pacing. The energy in the crowd is heightened, but not in a good way. Everyone looks agitated and anxious.

"Do you know what's going on down there?" Cooper calls out to George, who's still standing watch. "It's completely flooded, with at least a foot of water. No one's going home by car today."

The man in the business suit runs up to George and lines up with him nose-to-nose. "If that's true, it looks like you're going to have a car to pay for," he spits.

"Sir, I need you to take a step back and wait patiently while this is sorted out." George is calm and unruffled by the man in the suit, who turns and stomps over to us.

"How do you know this?" he demands.

"We found another stairwell. We saw it for ourselves," Cooper says.

"Take me there," the man says.

"I don't think it's a good idea," I say. "We could barely get through there with all the water. It's rushing in pretty quickly."

"Water is rushing in? What do you mean?" a woman asks. The group buzzes with comments and questions.

"I don't think it's just a water main break," Cooper says. "I mean, look at it outside. And my parents texted; they said that there's flooding and the bridge has been washed out."

"He's right," a middle-aged woman says. "It's breaking news." She holds up her phone to confirm it. Others start scrolling through their phones to read up on what's happening outside. Soon, most of the faces are lit up by the blue screens.

Gasps and a few cries of terror make the hair on my arms stand up. Suddenly I feel like the welfare of all of these people might be at stake, and the idea of harm coming to any of them makes me sick. As if on cue, the baby in the stroller starts to cry. It starts as a soft mew, but then it builds until it's a full-blown wail. The mother picks up the baby and tries rocking him, but nothing quiets him.

"He's hungry," she says. "I'm still nursing but he's been on solids for a while now and I didn't bring any extra food. I figured we'd be home long ago."

"Does anyone have any food they can give the baby?" George calls out to the crowd.

People rummage in their bags. Except for a ripe banana in the elderly woman's purse, there's nothing in the assortment of snacks they produce that the baby can eat. George takes the banana and makes a motion to throw it to me so that I can give it to her. I hold out my hands and hope for the best. I don't want to be responsible for starving this baby. The banana sails right into my outstretched hands and I pass it over to the woman.

"Thank you!" the mother says gratefully. I hold the stroller in place while she sets down the writhing, angry child. His face is almost purple from crying. He does not want to sit in his stroller. "Do you mind?" the woman asks as she peels the banana.

"What? You want me to hold him?" My eyes pop wide.

"Just for a sec?" she asks.

I do not want to be responsible for an injured baby and, truth be told, I don't have a clue how to hold a baby or what to do. I'm not sure this woman has thought things through. I scoop him up awkwardly and he stops crying for a moment to study me.

"You're just as surprised as I am, aren't you, little guy?" I talk to him. He blinks, his gaze never moving from my face. At least he isn't screaming at me.

"Who's got you? Who's got you now?" I say in a high voice I reserve for baby animals, and now, apparently, human babies. He coos at me for a moment and then breaks into a smile.

"You're a natural," comes a pretty voice. I look to my right and there she is. The goddess gamer. I tense up so tight I fear I'll drop the baby. She is casually scrolling through her phone.

"I have no idea what I'm doing," I admit. But for some reason, the baby keeps cooing and smiling at me.

"He seems to think you do," the girl says. The light illuminating her face allows me to see her perfectly aligned teeth. I want to keep making her smile just so I can see them over and over again.

"Thanks for making me look good!" I want to whisper to the kid. "You didn't make it out of the mall, eh?" I ask her.

"My car is downstairs. I guess according to you guys, it's more of a boat now?"

Cooper steps in. "Hi, I'm Cooper," he says, holding out his hand.

"Sam. Well, Samara," the girl says shaking his hand. I watch as their hands touch and I feel my stomach knot. How come he got to touch her and I'm stuck holding the baby?

The mother holds out a tiny piece of banana for the baby. I see that he has cute little baby teeth. He chomps down on the banana eagerly, drool cascading down his chin.

"Do you mind holding him while he eats?" the mother asks. "It's just you're so good with Ira, aren't you? You like him, don't you, Ira?" The mother's voice is melodic and soft and it makes Ira beam at her.

"Hi, Ira," I say. "I'm Zach."

"Thank you so much, Zach. I'm Valerie. I really appreciate your help. This is the last place I thought I'd be right now."

"No problem," I say gently. Ira is pretty cute, but he doesn't hold a candle to Samara, who's talking with Cooper. As much as I love my best friend, I don't want him to get to know Samara before I do.

TIP #3

Be a leader, not a follower

"Attention, everyone!" George yells. "I've got an update." Everybody stops talking and looks up at him expectantly. He clears his throat.

"The city is now experiencing flash flooding in some areas. We've got a pretty intense storm over us at the moment. I'm told that access to the underground lot is strictly denied. In fact, all entrances are being locked for the foreseeable future as it is unsafe to venture out of the building at this time."

"What about the bridge?" someone asks.

"It seems that the boys were right," he says, making eye contact with Cooper and me. "The bridge has been washed out due to flash flooding. They're saying that the only access point to this whole area is the grid road that heads north of the city. We're working on getting some power back on and stabilizing the facility for our safety."

The crowd grows loud as the information is digested.

"It's okay, Ira," Valerie soothes her son. "We're going to be just fine." She reaches out for Ira and I pass him over as gently as I can.

"Thanks again, Zach," she pats my arm. "I really appreciate it."

"Any time, right, little man?" I say to Ira. He smiles.

Now that my arms are free, I want to be beside Samara. She and Cooper are talking about something, and she throws her head back in laughter. I feel my stomach sink.

"Zach! Done babysitting?" Cooper asks.

"A man's gotta do what a man's gotta do," I say. "I'd say I saved the day there."

"Maybe we should call you the baby whisperer," Cooper jokes.

Samara smiles and touches me on the arm. "I thought it was very good of you to do that," she says seriously. My insides do a tumbling act.

"There's no way out of this place?" Chris asks, catching up to us.

"I'm afraid not," I tell him. "The bridge has been washed out and there's flash flooding. They're keeping us in here."

"Oh God. I just heard from Ali. She thinks she's in labour. I gotta find a way out of here."

"That sucks, man," Cooper says. I nod. I can't imagine being stuck in a building if my wife were in labour. I'd probably break a window and jump out.

"There *is* that grid road," I say.

Chris smiles and pats me on the back. "That's right! I forgot about that."

"Okay, everyone!" George calls out again. "I need all employees to make sure that their stores are secure, and that they have keys should we need them. Are there any employees from the food court here?"

Two hands shoot up.

"Where do you work?" George asks.

"Taco Time," a petite, greying woman answers. "My name's Olivia."

"The Coffee Hut," says a guy who looks to be twenty-five. "I'm Brandon."

"Let's all move and get settled in the food court. We'll find some drinks and see if we can't get some food for ourselves. It looks like we might be here a while." George makes sure the door to the stairwell is locked before motioning for us to walk.

The crowd shuffles together in the dark to get to the food court.

"How are we going to do this in the dark?" Olivia asks.

"We've got some flashlights. And I bet everyone here has an iPhone."

She fumbles with her key to pull open the metal covering on the restaurant front.

"Can you pull out all of the wraps and fresh veggies you have?" George asks.

"Yes, but it'll take a while," Olivia says.

"That's okay. We've got time," George says grimly. He shines his heavy-duty flashlight at the fridge.

Cooper jumps over the counter. He helps her empty the industrial-sized fridge. The woman with the middle-schoolers joins in.

"Nancy," she says, holding out her hand to Cooper and Olivia. They quickly shake it and introduce themselves.

"Do we want the beef and chicken?" Olivia asks.

"Yes. It'll keep us fuller longer. Who cares if it's cold," George replies.

George calls some people in the crowd to come and form an assembly line with Olivia.

"The rest of you can line up and we'll get everyone fed," George announces. "Can you go and check on Brandon?" he asks me.

I nod. I head toward the Coffee Hut.

I see Brandon standing at the counter but he's frozen in place.

"Hey, Brandon!" I exclaim as I approach. "Let's get things going over here."

He meets my eyes. "I don't really know what I'm doing here," he says. "That's a lot of people to take care of."

"It's okay," I say, calm. "You've got this. Just pretend it's first thing Saturday morning. You'd take care of a crowd like this in fifteen minutes flat."

"We don't have power."

"That's why this'll be easy. We just have to unload all of the drinks from the cooler."

Brandon nods, but he remains in place, staring blankly.

"C'mon. I'll help," I say. He follows me to the cooler but his hands are shaking uncontrollably.

"Dude, are you okay?" I ask. His face is drained of all colour.

"I ... I ..." He starts tearing up.

"Whoa, man, it's okay," I say, patting him on the back. "Let's just sit down."

Brandon starts breathing heavily.

"Deep breaths ... deep breaths ..." I say.

Instead of taking a chair, Brandon curls up in a ball on the floor.

"Just lie here," I say. "I've got this."

My palms are sweaty. If Brandon can't get it together, I'll have to take charge. I'm not the kind of guy to take control of a situation. I've never had that kind of confidence. I think of all of these people needing to be fed and kept safe. In strategy games, the player often has to manage resources, population, and construction. This situation is going to take strategy. Planning and skillful thinking. Quick decision-making. A plan to build up resources. Like in the storm that closes in on you in *Fortnite*.

"Is he okay?" It's Samara.

"I think he's having a panic attack," I tell her. "It's okay. I can get the drinks." I start working quickly.

"Here, let me help," Samara says, coming around the counter. The thought of working with her thrills me. I have to get to know this girl. She is magical.

Together we line up all of the drink choices on the front counter.

"I think if we put a few of each to start with and just replenish that drink as it's taken?" she suggests.

"Sounds great," I say. I turn to check on Brandon. He stays curled into himself but he seems to be breathing easier.

"Brandon, how are you doing?" He gives me a nod to let me know he's okay. I glance at the Taco Time. A group of people surround the counter holding up their phones for light so that Olivia and her new team can make the burritos. I decide to keep stacking drinks so that we're prepared for the onslaught of people. It's never good to be unprepared in a difficult situation.

Cooper is the first in line. "I don't want your ugly mug to serve me," he says.

"You shouldn't talk to girls like that," I quip. Cooper's eyes grow wide.

"You think I'm ugly?" Samara turns to me, feigning surprise.

I want to tell her that she's the most beautiful person I've ever seen, but Cooper isn't going to miss a beat when it comes to talking to her.

"Shall I compare thee to a summer's day? Thou art more lovely and more temperate …"

I roll my eyes.

"Shakespeare? C'mon," Samara groans. "What'll it be, Cooper?"

He reaches for a ginger ale and spins over to the end of the counter closest to Samara. Even though we're still technically in daylight hours, the light coming through the food court doors is pretty dim because of the storm.

"Can you come and light up this area for us?" I ask Cooper. He pulls out his phone from his pocket and aims the light toward the drink counter.

"Thanks, Coop," Samara says. She's calling him by his nickname already? How long have they known each other? Like, five minutes?

I have to check myself. I'm being ridiculous. I'm crushing on a girl I don't know and having raging jealousy when my best friend even looks at her. But her smile. Every time she laughs, her face lights up and her cheeks grow pink. The freckles on her nose wrinkle. Her emerald eyes practically sparkle, made all the more magical in the dim light of the iPhone flashlight. I am a goner.

The crowd has been given their burritos and soon we have a long lineup for drinks. Samara and I work quickly and efficiently together. Our hands bump a few times when grabbing drinks and I freeze each time and hope that she doesn't think I'm doing it on purpose. I mean, I want to hold her hand of course, but I'm not bumping her on purpose.

"Nice work, Zach," Samara says to me when the line ends. Our eyes meet but she quickly looks away. "Well, I'm going to go and get some food myself." She brushes her hands on her thighs and walks around me to get out from behind the counter.

I remember Brandon and check on him. He's sitting up now but he still looks a little dazed.

"Let's get you some food," I say. I help him up.

"It's all done?" he says, surprised.

"Sure is. All you need to do is rest."

He nods at me gratefully. He follows me to Taco Time.

Olivia is eating her own burrito but she puts it down as soon as she sees us.

"No, no, don't worry," I assure her. "We can make our own. Eat!"

She smiles and pats my cheek. "You're a good boy, Zach."

I blush. George or Chris must have told her my name. George continues to shine his flashlight on the food prep area. I look around as Brandon starts fixing himself a burrito. Cooper and Samara are sitting next to one another on a table. She's swinging her legs back and forth and smiling at Cooper. He's getting all the time with her and I am not.

Brandon and I finish making our food and join the rest of the people at the tables. It's weird eating with strangers in the semi-dark. Valerie and Ira are at the table next to us and she's feeding him bits of grated cheese and ground beef. He babbles and drools happily beside us, flashing his two front teeth.

"Is that going to be good enough for him?" I ask Valerie.

"Yeah, he'll be fine." Valerie smiles. "It's almost his bedtime. I'm hoping it'll help that the lights are out," she says ruefully.

Chris gazes over at Ira. He looks back at us.

"I have to find a way to Ali."

"Any updates?" I ask.

"No. But I can't get through to anyone at the moment," Chris says, studying his phone.

We all pull out our phones.

"I don't have service," Samara notices.

"I can't get through!" Nancy says. "I've got no service!"

Others study their phones. Sure enough, there isn't any cell service anymore. "It's probably because of the storm," George assures us. "I'm sure they'll have us up and running again in no time. Lots of people are probably trying to get through at once."

He talks into his radio and soon two other security guards join us.

"The mall is all clear," one of them announces. He's a tall, lanky guard who doesn't look much older than me. His face is full of pockmarks, likely from acne. He certainly doesn't look capable of saving us from any real danger. The other guard is an older gentleman, likely retirement age with white hair and a thin white moustache; he's fairly short and has a pot belly. I know it sounds stereotypical but my instincts are telling me I'll be relying on George for any real security.

"Okay, we're the last ones in the mall. This is Rory and Erwin," says George. Rory is the tall one, and Erwin is the short one. "And I've just done a head count. There are thirty-two of us. I want us to stick together at all times. Unless you need to use the washrooms of course — which are right over there ..." George points to the corridor where the washrooms are. "The police know that we're here. They're figuring out the best course of action. So we're just going to have to sit tight for now. Get comfortable. It may be a while."

People groan. Valerie wipes Ira's face. "Do you mind watching the stroller while I go and change him?" she asks

me. She slings a diaper bag over her shoulder and has Ira
in her other arm.

"No problem," I say. "Are you going to be okay without
the lights?"

"I've got my phone like everyone else," Valerie says,
chuckling. "I think I'll be fine."

"Are you going to be Ira's new daddy?" Cooper jokes
when they walk away. Samara laughs and spits out some of
her drink. I feel a surge of anger at Coop's words.

"Ha, ha," I mutter.

"I'm going to go to the washroom," Samara announces.

"I have to go, too. I'll walk with you," Cooper says,
following on her heels. I watch the two of them walk away
together. Of course, the two of them have to hold on to
each other to find their way through the dark. Chris sees
my eyes narrow.

"You okay, Zach?" he asks, looking back and forth from
me to Cooper.

"Fine." I sigh.

"Is it the girl?" he asks.

"Is it that obvious?" I scrunch my face.

"Only to me, I bet," Chris says quietly. He leans in
closer. "Can I tell you something?"

I nod.

"I mean, I feel like I've known you guys quite a
while now," Chris whispers. It's true. We've been going
to Gamer's Haven faithfully for several years now.
Our parents started bringing us to the original store
in the rundown strip mall not too far from my house

after Cooper got a PlayStation 3 and I got a Wii the Christmas we were ten. Chris moved the store into the new mall when it opened and, even though it was farther from both of us, we felt like we had to keep supporting both our habits and Chris by visiting the new location. I bet we were among his best customers. "She's a pretty girl, there's no doubt about that. Cooper's a nice kid and all … but don't count yourself out just yet." He stands up to empty his tray in the garbage before I can say anything back. The truth is, I am pretty speechless. Valerie and Ira return and Ira's eyelids are already fluttering.

"Thank you so much, Zach. I can't thank you enough for being so sweet. I've really appreciated the help." She sets Ira in the stroller and covers him with a plush yellow blanket. He looks so tiny and innocent.

"No problem, Valerie. I just hope you guys get to go home as soon as possible. It's no fun being stuck in here."

"Well, that bridge being out sure makes things tricky. But I'm sure it won't be too long. And I'd rather be in here than out there," she says. I nod. Sure, the power is out, but as far as I can tell, we'll be safest here.

"Might as well make the best of it," I say. Cooper and Samara come ambling out from the washrooms and slowly make their way back to the tables. She's smiling at something he has said. That's Coop. Always trying to crack jokes and be witty. I watch as he slings his arm around her shoulder for a brief moment and then takes it off. Maybe he's worried he's going too far, but Samara doesn't seem to mind. They stare out the food court entrance doors from about twenty feet away. It is ugly out there. The doors rattle from the wind and the rain. Everyone sits in an unnerving silence, listening to the storm batter the building. There are creaks and bangs happening at random, and being in the semi-dark intensifies the creepiness of it all. Samara rubs her arms and then takes her scarf from around her neck and wraps it around her arms like a shawl. She and Cooper venture back to the table but keep glancing outside nervously.

"Guess I'm not going out for my mom's birthday," Cooper says.

A loud crack gives everyone a startle, and then almost without warning the glass from the food court entrance explodes and tiny diamond-like shards of glass blast through the air, blanketing the floor just beyond where we're sitting. The sound is deafening; many people scream and cover their ears. Samara leaps toward me. I hold my arm over her protectively. The middle-schoolers start crying, and the elderly woman grabs on to her husband. Ira wakes with a start and starts crying along with them. Valerie holds him so tightly to her chest, I worry about how scared she is, too. Wind whips through the opening, whistling so loudly that we have to keep our ears covered. Water cascades through the door, slowly at first, but then it starts to pour through at a quicker pace. My heart thunders in my chest.

"Are you okay?" I ask Samara. I'm shocked that she's ended up in my arms. She nods but keeps her arms crossed protectively in front of her. I take my arm off of her. It was probably a fluke — a knee-jerk reaction from fear.

George springs to his feet. "I need everyone to head back to the middle of the mall where the elevators are," he says. "Let's try to take any of the remaining drinks and food items with us. If we all work together we'll be able to do this quickly and efficiently."

Most of the people stand still, taking in the scene before them. Water pushes the glass farther into the building, and the wind is so strong and cold that it feels like we aren't in a building at all.

We can't stay in this area. It isn't safe … but nobody moves. Being put in a difficult situation forces you to use your wits to figure out how to succeed. I think of how in *Fortnite* your team has to work together. You have to plan where to drop, and you have to do it quickly and together, otherwise you can't help each other when things get rough. We've got to stick together.

"Follow me!" I yell, hoping that people will follow. Chris, Cooper, Samara, and Valerie and Ira eagerly follow me out, hoping to get somewhere safer. Slowly, others start to follow.

As we make our way out of the food court, George and the other security guards scramble to find something to cover the broken entrance to keep the elements out. The water isn't going to stop coming in.

"We have to find a way to secure this entrance," George yells to Rory and Erwin. "Find what you can."

"We've got this," Rory says to him. "You go with the others. We'll catch up."

"Are you sure?" George looks back and forth from the blown-out door to the rest of us. I can see he's reached a moment: a pivotal decision must be made. Do you remain with your team? Is there strength in numbers? George takes a deep breath and joins the rest of us.

We shuffle back to the elevators, each of us carrying drinks or food items in case we need them for our next meal. Brandon's pulling a cooler that's been filled with the remaining food from Taco Time.

"We'll be safer in the middle," I say.

"Are you sure about that?" Cooper yells, pointing to the door to the stairwell that George had locked earlier.

We all shine our lights toward the door, and sure enough, water is lapping at the base of it ever so slowly, like a tide coming in and out. George looks down through the little window in the door, and his face turns white. He reports that the water is coming up from underground now, which means that the parking lot is completely flooded.

The man in the suit starts swearing and kicks the metal garbage can, making the elderly couple jump.

Erwin and Rory appear.

"Did you get that door secured?" George asks. He's wiping sweat from his brow.

"As best we could for now," Rory says. "It's not like we had a lot to work with."

"As long as it keeps the elements out for a while."

"Maybe we should be more worried about what's coming in." Edwin points to the door as he sees the water for the first time.

"I know," George says. "It doesn't look good."

The three guards shine their lights around our surroundings until they land on the escalators nearby.

"New plan," Erwin says. "We're heading upstairs."

TIP #4

"Aren't you supposed to go lower if there's a tornado?"
I mutter. By going up to the second floor in a building
with a glass roof, I can't help but think we are practically
bullfighting, daring this possible tornado to come after us.
Apparently, I'm not the only one.

"Is this a good idea?" the elderly gentleman says. "I
remember back in 2007 there was an F5 tornado. No
people died, but my sister's dog Ginger was killed in
that storm."

"I understand what you're saying, but the tornado's a
long way off yet, and we should be able to leave before we
have to worry about it," Erwin says.

"That tornado was in Elie, Manitoba," the man says to
no one in particular.

George strokes his chin and looks around intently.
"Change of plans," he announces.

"What do you mean?" Erwin bellows.

"He's right. Heading higher isn't safe if there's a tornado warning. We need to stay down here."

Erwin shakes his head and fumes. "So, what? Staying where there's water coming in is going to be safer?"

"For now, yes," George says pointedly. "We don't know how close that tornado is. We're better off staying in the centre of the mall. If the water becomes a serious problem, we re-evaluate."

"I disagree," says Erwin.

"Well, I'm the senior officer in charge here. I say we stay here."

What are the chances that the mall will actually flood anyhow? It doesn't seem logical.

The sound of water lapping at the bottom of the door distracts me. In a steady rhythm, it crawls out a little farther with every lap, like fingers stretching out, threatening to grab us. Just how much rain is there? How bad could things get? How could things have gotten so out of control when just hours ago it was a harmless rainy day?

"Maybe we should ask them," Rory pipes in. He turns to the crowd. "By show of hands, who wants to stay here and who thinks we should head upstairs?"

All eyes turn to the lapping water at the door. Going upstairs feels safer at the moment.

"Upstairs!" Nancy glances at Liam and Henry and many people murmur in agreement.

"Is that what you all want to do?" asks George. Hands shoot up in quick succession. "I guess we're heading upstairs then." He sighs.

"Sounds good to me," Cooper says.

George speaks through his radio but he's just far enough from the group that all I can hear is muffled static.

"So … it's just a matter of waiting out the storm?" I ask no one in particular.

"I guess," Samara replies.

"Were you here by yourself?" Cooper asks her, suddenly surprised at the realization.

"Yes. Is that a problem?" Samara challenges.

"No, not at all!" Cooper put his hands up. "Just used to seeing girls in packs all of the time."

Samara scoffs. "I'm pretty independent."

Cooper nods and breaks out into a huge smile. He's falling for her, too. I can see it all over his face.

"That's cool," I say. It is. Even though I don't know her at all, so far everything I'm learning about this girl is thrilling to me. She's unlike any other girl I've ever met — not that I'm someone who is meeting girls left and right, but she just seems different. Cooler.

"How long do you think we'll be here?" Samara asks. Coop and I shrug. I can't see how we'd be stuck for long. Storms generally pass by pretty quickly. This is all precaution as far as I can tell.

"I could have been eating a New York steak with grilled mushrooms and those french-fried onions they put on top," Cooper muses. The thought of it makes my own stomach growl.

"Not me. My dad was cooking fish." I scrunch up my nose. I hate all forms of seafood, so I won't be missing out.

"Your fave." Cooper laughs and turns to Samara. "What about you?"

She's playing with her thick ponytail, twirling it in her fingers. More wisps of her rich, red-tinged hair fall loose. I imagine what she looks like with that silky mound of hair unravelled around her. She'd look like Sophie Turner playing Jean Grey in *X-Men: Apocalypse*. My cheeks grow hot. I look away.

"Oh, you know. A full turkey dinner with all of the fixings."

"Wow. It isn't even Thanksgiving or anything. Lucky," Cooper says.

"Sure. My mom can cook anything," Samara says with a shrug.

- - - -

The only way to the second floor is the escalators frozen in place on either side of the mall. Seeing that, Valerie's face tightens.

"It's okay, we'll carry the stroller up for you," I assure her. She looks worn out. Her eyes hold a worry in them I hadn't seen earlier. Ira is fast asleep in the stroller, the yellow blanket stuffed into his fists. She scoops him up in her arms gingerly, careful not to wake him.

A couple of women in dress clothes with gold name tags on are taking off their heels to climb the escalator. George asks them where they work.

"Designer Dresses, on the second floor," one says. They are both in their twenties, and the two of them look terrified.

"Do you have keys?" George asks.

"Right here," one of them says, holding out an elastic wristband with a key ring attached. George nods and continues talking with them while Cooper and I each take one end of Ira's stroller and walk it up the stairs, careful not to trip since we're only being guided by the limited light of our phones. Valerie follows us with Ira in her arms, but she seems tired and drawn out.

"Thanks again," she says to us, placing the baby gently back into the stroller before pushing it over to the railing and taking a seat on the floor as everyone else arrives.

One by one, everyone makes their way to the top.

"Where's Chris?" Cooper asks. Samara, Cooper, and I look around for him but we can't spot him.

"Did you see a guy in his thirties, short sandy-brown hair? Wearing a Punisher T-shirt and jeans?" Cooper starts asking people. People either shake their heads or answer with, "What's a Punisher T-shirt?" We're worried that Chris has run off. With his wife having a baby, would he have waited until everyone was occupied and then snuck away? I hope he just went back to the store to retrieve something.

I look around for George. He's on his way up the escalator, carrying the elderly woman in his arms. Her face is worn with more than time. She clutches George's collar for dear life as he brings her up. Her husband follows behind them, reassuring his wife.

"It'll be okay, Mildred," he soothes. He's carrying her sweater in one arm and holding the handrail with the

other. He moves slowly but he has a steadiness about him
that makes me think he's an excellent caregiver to his wife.

George puts Mildred down. She smooths her blue
slacks and her snow-white curls before reaching for her
sweater from her husband.

"Peter, I'm scared." She starts to cry again.

"Shhh … it's okay, Millie. We're going to be just fine.
They'll have us out of here before you know it."

He pulls her toward him and she crumples in his arms.
"I'm not sure I'm strong enough to last," she says through
her tears.

"Well, of course you are, my dear. I'm right here, and
look at all of these people. We will all keep each other
safe." Peter looks up at Cooper and me and we both nod
with polite smiles.

"Will it be like when Farrah died?" Mildred asks.

"What? What do you mean?" Peter steps back to look
at his wife's face.

"Are we going to die like Farrah did?" Her eyes are wild
with fear. Peter searches his wife's face, trying to compute
what she's saying.

"Farrah? No, my dear. We'll be rescued soon. We have
nothing to worry about. What happened to Farrah was
an accident."

Mildred weeps uncontrollably. George pats Peter on
the shoulder. "Is she okay? She's not hurt, is she?" George
looks her over, clearly hoping he hasn't hurt her while he
carried her up.

"No. She's just scared, I think."

"Farrah," Mildred says softly, rocking back and forth.

"Our daughter," Peter says to George, his eyes filling with tears. "She drowned when she was a child. Millie seems to think that we're about to drown, too."

"Ma'am, we're going to get everyone out of here safely," George assures her. Mildred nods, but it's clear that she doesn't quite believe him.

"Can we get another head count please?" George calls out. Everyone sits on the tiled landing at the top of the escalators. George counts. "That's odd," he says, and he counts the heads once more. "According to my count, we're missing three."

I swallow hard. We were all supposed to stick together. We have to. Any time or resources spent looking for people is going to take away from the group's overall safety. Any gamer knows that.

"Who are we missing?" Rory asks.

"Those two guys … the ones in the track suits," George realizes. "And Chris."

An uneasiness comes over the group. Why would people walk off? And if the security guards leave to go and look for them, will they come back? Will the group be safe? The guards have radios, which have enabled contact with the outside world. Without them, how will we know when and where to go to get rescued?

"I'll go check the store," I offer. George shakes his head.

"No, everybody has to stay here." He's deep in thought. He surveys the group.

Peter is still holding Mildred. Her face is buried in his chest but her shoulders shake and she keeps sniffling in loud bursts. Peter caresses his wife's back, but his eyes hold the same kind of worry I've just witnessed in Valerie's eyes. It's as though the water seeping into the main floor has changed everything. There's a new element of danger and going upstairs added a new complication to our rescue.

I don't want to think too much about the rising water. It seems nearly impossible that the water could get very high before we get out of here. It's not like Saskatoon has ever experienced the kind of storms that have people being rescued by boat like you see in the movies or in some places in the United States. Sure, there's flooding, but usually it drains pretty quickly once the storm sewers can catch up. At most, there's some property damage.

The storm will subside, or at the very least, the police and rescue teams will figure out the best way to get us. We won't be able to go long without food or water, so they'll have to come up with a plan quickly. We have a baby here, and that has to constitute a real emergency. Babies are a special case in any crisis if you ask me.

Ira is still sleeping soundly. Valerie sits beside the stroller with one arm draped over his blanketed figure but her eyes are focused intently on the ceiling. On a good day, the glass ceiling illuminates the second floor in a brilliant display of unfiltered sunlight. Today splats of rain coat the slate-grey glass that looms over us. Added to the fact that it's now dusk, the colour is ominous.

"I'll go," Rory offers. "I know who he is. I bought *Mario Kart 8* from him for my little brother's birthday."

George nods. "Okay, just keep in touch if you can." He checks his radio again. "My battery's getting low. What are the chances you could try to snag the remaining ones from the office?"

"Can't see it being a problem," Rory says. He puffs his chest out as though the task will be effortless. Rory wasn't down in that part of the mall when Cooper and I were there, though. The security office was near the underground parking exit that we tried. Even then the water was rising fast. I wonder if he even has a chance of getting near those offices now.

We all watch as Rory tears down the escalator stairs, which remain frozen in place.

"He thinks it'll be easy, but five bucks says he's back within a minute," I whisper to Coop.

"Okay everyone," George calls out again. Tufts of his damp, dark hair stick out from under his black duty cap. Beads of sweat trickle down his temples. "We're going to head into Designer Dresses. There's carpet in there at least and stuff we can use for pillows and blankets if we need to."

Everyone stares back blankly. It feels like I'm dreaming and that none of this is actually real. The two ladies reluctantly unlock and pull open the security gates in front of the store. They don't look comfortable with the group of us using the store as our headquarters. George pulls the puffiest dress he can find and slips it off of its hanger.

"Peter, why don't we let Mildred rest here," he says, huffing and puffing as he lays the dress out like a blanket.

One of the sales women gasps as she watches Peter lead Mildred to the pink satin and help her down onto the expensive dress. "I don't feel good about this," she admits. "I'm going to lose my job." She wrings her hands.

The other sales woman turns to her co-worker and shrugs. "We have no idea how long we'll be stuck in the building," she says. No one expected us to be bunking down in the most expensive store in the mall besides the jewellery store, but she's right — we have to do something to keep everyone warm and comfortable.

"Listen," says George, "anything we use in the mall while we're here will not affect your employment. You've been advised by me to do all of these things because we're in a crisis situation. It's my duty to ensure the safety of both your lives and the building itself. I'm responding to this event as I deem necessary in order to maintain the greatest level of safety I can based on the knowledge I have at any given time. This is a special circumstance, as you can well see."

I watch as Cooper pulls a poufy navy dress off of a rack and lays it out for Samara. He holds his arms out toward it, motioning for her to have a seat. She smiles and plunks down on it, cross-legged, the layers of gauzy fabric puffing up around her legs. Cooper quickly joins her. I feel another pang of jealousy. There definitely isn't room on that dress for three.

Valerie is struggling with the stroller as she holds Ira in her arms. I take over for her and push the stroller to a wide expanse of carpet. I choose a fuchsia ball gown from the nearest rack and lay it down like George and Cooper did with the others. I motion for Valerie to have a seat, and she giggles.

"Thanks, Zach. You're a sweetheart!" She seems genuinely touched that I'm helping her. I don't want Valerie to see my disappointment, but I wish Samara were the one gushing at me. How did I end up helping a woman with a baby instead of the cute girl my age? And how did Cooper become the one to help her when I was clearly the one who was interested in her first?

Cooper has always been more outgoing than me. He has a way of making friends with anybody — and that's something I struggle with. I tend to keep to myself. Cooper has always been the kind of guy who can walk into a room and confidently talk to anyone. He's not worried about cliques or about not being accepted. He goes about life with a "take me or leave me" attitude, which is something I definitely don't have. I worry too much about people making fun of me or thinking I'm a loser when I enter a room full of people.

From the moment I missed the last shot in our final Grade 7 junior-team game, a kid named Josh Logan made my life a living hell. He decided that I wasn't fit to play basketball before school anymore, and he had most of the guys shaking their heads and ignoring me whenever I came around. In the ten seconds it took for me to get across the court, throw the shot, and then miss it, I became a social leper of epic proportions at Hollander Elementary.

Josh threw spitballs at me on the bus, put his foot out to trip me — basically anything to make me feel like I was two inches tall. He seemed to forget that I had been the one to help him get to school practically every day in Grades 3 to 5 when his anxiety had started getting the best of him and he wasn't sure he could make it into school by himself anymore. Now I'd become the target of his preteen rage. After that, I started shrinking. Shrinking from friends, shrinking from new things, shrinking from myself.

My ability to enter a room and not think or care about what others thought of me died with that fateful basketball shot. Somehow being me wasn't cutting it anymore in the real world, and so I got better at trying to make myself as invisible as possible so that I wouldn't have to feel the sting of rejection.

Maybe that's why I retreated so far into video games. Besides tucking myself away for hours at a time and being able to zone out, gaming allowed me to have some control. I could decide my destiny and come out on top again. I could fight in a way that left others in awe of my abilities instead of living the reality of being a total wimp whenever Josh Logan was around.

Even though we're almost in Grade 11 now, the effects of Josh's wrath haven't even become a scar yet. I barely have any contact with him anymore (one of the great things about high school is blending in among three hundred students in my grade rather than the fifty students in my grade in elementary school) but even picturing him or replaying his voice in my head makes me ache all over again, the wounds freshly open. Sure, they're trying to scab over and heal, but every so often I replay the events in my head and it feels like I'm ripping them all open again.

"Hey, I want to sit here!" one of the middle-schoolers yells. "Can't you hear me?!" He's waving his arms in front of Brandon.

"Heelllllloooo?" the other kid says.

I rush over. "What's going on?"

"This dude won't move. He's just sitting here like an idiot ..." The kid is making faces at Brandon and trying to get his attention.

"Hey," I interject. "Don't talk to people like that!" The boys both roll their eyes.

I kneel down beside Brandon, who doesn't even look up at us. Instead he's focused on a spot on the ground. His arms are tucked around his knees and he is rocking back and forth slowly. He's having another panic attack. My heart surges with compassion for him. His face is pale and clearly strained. Whatever he's dealing with is not easy.

"Brandon — you okay?" I ask gently. He blinks but doesn't meet my eyes. The two boys stand over us with their hands on their hips as though they fully expect us to clear out for them. "Where is your mom?" I ask pointedly. The boys both falter a bit from their tough guy stances. "Seriously. Scram!" I bark. The last thing Brandon needs is some punk kids with attitudes making fun of him. His distress is unsettling to me — I can't imagine how he's feeling.

"Thanks," Brandon whispers when the boys trot off.

"What can I do? I don't know how to help," I admit. We sit in silence for a minute or two.

"Do you mind just hanging out here for a few minutes?" Brandon says softly.

"No problem," I say.

"Maybe just make small talk for a while?" Brandon asks. I look over at his face and see tears forming in his eyes. He seems embarrassed.

"It's all good, man," I assure him. "How long have you been working at the Coffee Hut for?"

"About a year," he replies. He stops rocking and just holds his legs tightly against himself.

"Cool. I can't wait to get a job. I've been training to be a lifeguard," I say. Brandon doesn't answer. "I can't wait to have some extra cash. Plus, I'll get to work with girls in bathing suits all day." When he smiles, it feels like a victory.

"I think my car is destroyed," he mutters. "It was underground."

"Yeah. Me and my friend Cooper were down there — it didn't look good," I confirm. "It could be worse. I think that guy lost his Porsche Cayenne." I lean toward him and nod over at the man in the business suit. He's pacing outside of the store with his permanent scowl lit up by the light of his phone. He's jabbing repeatedly at it, like he's trying to text or phone somebody, which is obviously not working. Brandon lets out a low whistle.

"Ouch," he says.

"Plus, I'm pretty sure that he's not going to rest on one of these fluffy dresses under any circumstance. He probably sleeps standing up anyhow." The man is wound so tightly, I wonder if he'll explode.

It's ridiculous that we're sitting in the dark on these dresses on the floor of a retail store in the middle of a raging storm. A quick glance around the store reveals candy-coloured dresses dotted across the carpet and multiple faces glowing blue from the light of people's phones. Brandon laughs and unhooks his arms so he can stretch his legs. I take that as a sign that he's relaxing.

"I get these stupid panic attacks," Brandon says softly. "They make my life hell."

I nod.

"Something like the world possibly ending doesn't help," he says.

"Nah, we're going to be fine," I assure him. "We'll be out of here before you know it. But yeah, they don't seem very fun …"

"Thanks for hanging out with me for a bit."

"For sure. Any time."

Brandon takes a long swig from the bottled water he has with him. He seems to be doing a lot better. I pat him on the shoulder. I notice sparkles on my pants from the dress we're sitting on. I brush them off and my eyes catch the price tag that I've bent by sitting on it.

"By the way, you're sitting on a nine-hundred-dollar dress," I tease, pointing to the tag.

"Maybe I can sell it to buy a new car," Brandon says wryly.

"Why? Hot pink's not your colour?"

Brandon grins. "You're all right, Zach."

"I try," I say, smiling back. "I'll check back in a bit."

I spot the boys in the corner of the store. They're sitting under a rack of dresses almost out of sight. I head over.

"Treating people like that will get you nowhere," I say, bending over to make eye contact with them.

"The guy's a freak," one of them says.

"No, he isn't. And acting like jerks makes you guys look like the freaks."

"We wanted to sit there," the other one says, laughing.

My fists ball up and sweat starts to form on my forehead. I want to take a swing at these two kids but how would that look? A fifteen-year-old slugging an eleven- or twelve-year-old? I feel like they're two Josh Logans in the making, and I've had enough of one Josh Logan for a lifetime.

"Look, you rat punks — if I see you so much as utter a syllable that isn't nice to someone here, I'll knock your teeth out," I say, seething.

For once the boys actually stay silent. A little thrill runs through me. I've never talked to anyone like that before. I've always been too scared. Too scared to "rock the boat" any more than it's already rocking. This time I feel full and charged. I feel powerful. It feels like not only am I standing up for Brandon, but in a weird way, I'm standing up for my younger self, too. Enough is enough.

TIP 85

Samara and Cooper are deep in conversation and scrolling through their phones when I make it back to them. They both look up at the same time and seem happy to see me.

"Come, have a seat," Cooper says, scooting closer to Samara and opening up a spot for me farthest from her. I want to shift the opposite way and get closer to her but I figure these two are probably already so into each other that I no longer stand a chance.

"Where've you been?" Cooper asks.

"Oh, you know ... here and there," I say vaguely. I don't want to tell them about Brandon's panic attack.

"We missed you," Samara says. I smile but don't know what to say next.

"I wonder if that guy found Chris," Cooper says. I nod.

We sit in awkward silence.

"I was telling Samara about how my parents want me to be a lawyer just like them," Cooper says finally. "It turns out her parents are lawyers, too."

"Both of them?" I manage.

Samara nods. "They even practise the same kind of law as Cooper's parents. They probably know each other." Samara and Cooper are practically beaming at each other. Great. Their parents are old pals and soon Cooper will be part of the same club. He'll make the perfect son-in-law.

"What do your parents do?" Samara asks me.

"My dad runs a printing business and my mom works at a care home," I say.

"That's cool," Samara says. "I'd love to have my own business someday."

"It's nothing big, really. Just a little place." It's no match for a lawyer. I'm sure she'll see that Cooper would be the better choice — the better provider for their future family. I look at Cooper and he just looks happy. It makes me feel sick.

"Zach's parents want him to become a doctor," Cooper says. It's true. "And he's wanted to be one for pretty much forever." Ever since I had surgery on a broken leg in Grade 4, I've been pretty enthralled with medicine. Seeing that interest fuelled my parents into sending me to every STEM camp imaginable in the hopes that I'd get amazing science grades in preparation for school. I'd argue with them that technically marks didn't count much until Grade 10, as that's when they go on your high school transcript (and if we're being really technical, the marks don't really count until university when it's time to apply for medical school), but they never listened.

"Now that I am getting older, I'm not so sure anymore," I tell Samara. "I mean, I'm still fascinated by medicine, but I'm not sure I have what it takes to get through the program."

"You're one of the smartest guys I know," Cooper says. "And one of the best gamers."

I can't help but smile. For Coop to admit that I'm a pretty good gamer is a big deal. We're pretty competitive when it comes to gaming. Far more than when it comes to our grades.

"What kind of business do you want to open?" I ask, changing the subject.

"I'd like to design shoes," Samara says shyly. I look down at her purple suede knee-high boots and smile. They're a bold choice so I guess I'm not too surprised. I've never seen anyone wear anything like them. They draw attention to her legs, though, and I feel my cheeks get hot as I study her legs at the same time.

"Makes sense." I nod, trying to be imperceptible so she doesn't think I'm a creep.

"Do you like my boots?" she asks me pointedly. Her legs would look good in any way, shape, or form but I can't tell her that. The boots are sexy as hell with her denim skirt, but I don't know how to answer. There's the automatic answer swimming in my head and the more gentlemanly answer I need time to formulate.

"Yeah. They're great," I manage. "They look pretty stylish." I want to add that's it's the woman that makes the boots, not the boots that make the woman, but I don't have the guts.

"Thanks. They're my favourite. I got them from the thrift store downtown."

Cooper and I both nod while she talks.

"I've been sketching things most of my life," she explains, pulling out a notebook from her crossbody bag. She shines the flashlight from her phone over the pages and flips through the book slowly so we can have a look at some of her work. It's mostly anime. It's fantastic.

"You've got skills." I whistle. Most of the characters she's drawn are wearing simple non-descript clothing. It's the footwear that gets all of the attention.

"Thanks, Zach." She looks down at the ground and blushes. "I'd like to get into art and design school but my parents think it's a dead-end career. They don't really get the whole art thing. They'd rather I go into law, too. My mom has this fantasy that we could all work together in the same building like one happy family." She rolls her eyes.

"Do you have siblings?" I ask. She shakes her head no.

"I'm an only child, too!" Cooper pipes up. The two of them high-five and laugh about another similarity between them.

"How about you, Cooper?" Samara asks. "Are you thinking of law like your parents?"

"They really want me to," Cooper says. "I just kind of assumed that it would be my path, too. It interests me enough."

"That's cool." Samara grows silent. We look around the store. Many faces glow blue from the light from their screens. Other than a few low-volume conversations, it's pretty quiet.

I get to thinking about my parents. I think of how hard my dad is working to get my new room done. He's been spending every night in the basement from the moment he gets home until late at night. He isn't a carpenter by any means, so he has to really research every step. He's a perfectionist so I know it's taking so long because he wants everything to be just right. The thought of him down there, a pencil hanging from his lips as he measures and remeasures, gives me pangs in my heart. My parents have always wanted the best for me. I've been lucky. They aren't even that annoying as far as parents go. I got a pretty good deal. They try to spend as much time with Marshall and me as they can. I know Cooper's parents are a lot more distant. They don't have as much time, and so they try to make up for it with money.

Cooper must be thinking of his parents, too.

"I wonder where my parents are," he says. "I wonder if they're still in their car or if they turned around and went home."

"I can't believe the bridge got washed out," I say. This mall just opened a year ago. The bridge and the whole development was new then. It's hard to imagine that this storm that no one really saw coming could take the bridge out like that.

"I hope they're safe," Cooper says softly.

I pat him on the shoulder. "For sure, man. They're safe." We both check our phones just in case something has changed. Nothing has. I think of my own parents and what they're probably doing. Marshall would be home from baseball practice — if he got to have one, that is, given the storm. Do they even know I'm here? Cooper's parents know we're stuck here and they've probably called my parents. I'm kind of surprised my dad's not trying to bust through the door right now to find me. That's the kind of dad he is, always wanting his family together for everything. I picture him outside, ready to spot any movement within so that he can rescue me.

Then it hits me that maybe they're not safe. What if the storm has hit near home in ways that are even worse than here? My insides tighten.

Just keep calm, I tell myself. *Everything is going to be okay.*

"Get back here!" George's voice is shrill and it startles most of us. He's calling down the escalator at someone. Cooper and I jump to our feet to see what's happening.

"We'll all be safer if we stay together!" George yells. It's the man in the business suit, his balding scalp the only contrast from his black hair and charcoal suit.

"Let him go. The guy seems like a real jerk anyway," Cooper mutters.

"How hard is it to follow a few simple rules?" George continues. "We can't be chasing people all around the mall. I have a duty to keep everyone safe." He wipes sweat from his forehead and shakes his head. He aims his flashlight back at our feet.

"Want us to go after him?" I ask.

George shakes his head again. "No, the last thing I need is to lose the two of you. You've been an enormous help to me," he says, looking me hard in the eyes. I feel a little surge of pride, even though it feels like we really haven't done anything.

"Now that's four missing." George's eyes are dark. "How is everyone else doing?"

"I think they're managing all right," I say. I think of Mildred crying and Brandon having another panic attack. "I mean, all things considered."

George turns back toward Designer Dresses.

"Okay, everyone. Listen up! We've got washrooms to our left here." He points to a corridor two stores down. "You are not to go past that corridor, please! If you require assistance to get to the washrooms, those of us with lights can take you there. We want to stay in this area together. Hopefully we'll all be heading home before dark tonight — ba dum bump!" George mimes a drummer's rimshot. "Pardon the pun. But if we don't get out tonight, this is as good a place to sleep as any. Bet you've never slept in luxury fabrics like these before." He cracks a smile but no one laughs. "I continue to be in touch with law enforcement and they are working to get to us."

There are a few sighs of relief. The air feels charged — though I can't tell how much of it is from the group and how much of it is from the weather outside. There's a definite energy circling around us. The way this large building is rattling and creaking from the wind is eerie and ominous. It's like the storm stole the electricity and used it to supercharge itself. It reminds me of the docile, regular-looking Dr. Bruce Banner from my Marvel comics: *"Caught in the blast of gamma radiation, brilliant scientist Bruce Banner is cursed to transform in times of stress into the living engine of destruction known as THE INCREDIBLE HULK."*

"You're deep in thought," Samara says. "Whatcha thinking about?"

I laugh. "Would it be weird if I said I was comparing the storm to the Incredible Hulk?"

"Not at all. He's a menace that unleashes his power onto others without thought."

"Well, I don't know about that. He's a genius."

"No, Bruce Banner is a genius. The Hulk is a crazed behemoth. They had to merge their psyches in order for him to get a hold of himself."

"You read the comics?" I ask incredulously.

"Again — is that a problem? You seem pretty hung up on me being into this stuff."

"I've just never met anyone like you before," I say, my jaw hanging loosely as I try to process our conversation.

"Since I don't know what you mean by that exactly, I think I should go and see if I can be of any help around here." Samara stands up quickly, smooths down her skirt, and then walks off toward George. She's upset. I close my eyes and berate myself. I didn't mean to insult her in any way, but she obviously thinks I'm judging her somehow. What she must not understand is just how awesome I think it is that she likes the same stuff as I do. I'm obviously not getting across to her how awesome I think she is.

"This is when we need Chris," Cooper says. "He could unlock the store and we could play games all night. And forget moody girls."

"Not without power," I remind him.

"Aw, yeah. I keep forgetting that part." Cooper looks at his phone. "How much power do you have left on your phone?"

I dig mine out of my pocket. "Thirty-seven percent. You?"

Cooper whistles. "I'm down to eight."

My stomach lurches again at the thought of all of our phones going dead and having no way to charge them. "Surely the power will be back on soon. It's already been a couple of hours, hasn't it?"

"Yeah, I think so."

"What I wouldn't do for a bag of Nacho Cheese Doritos and a Big Gulp right now."

"I could go for that," Cooper agrees. "Looks like we'll be missing our game tonight."

Since we started our team six months ago, we've never missed a night of playing *Fortnite*. We established an awesome squad on Discord — we all got Battle Passes and we levelled up fast so people are always looking to join us. We consider ourselves to be pretty good. Not Epic Games-tournament worthy, but definitely worth our salt. I usually stopped by the 7-Eleven near my house before our game time to get some munchies. We'd be starting in a few minutes if we were at home. No wonder I was craving my cheese fix.

Samara makes her way back to us. "I guess they don't need me for anything." She flops down beside us.

"Look, if I said something that upset you —" I start but she interrupts me.

"Is this a gender issue with you or something, Zach? Did you know that over forty percent of gamers are female? Did you know that we make up almost half of the industry these days?"

"I think the fact that you are into gaming and comics is the coolest thing I've ever heard!" I tell her. "Serious! It's awesome!"

"I feel like you're making fun of me. Like I'm not cool enough for you or something."

God, if she only knew. She was so out of my league that I could barely talk around her. It's why I was messing everything up.

"Do you play *Fortnite?*" Cooper asks.

"Yeah. Who doesn't?" Samara says, shooting me a dirty look.

"*Battle Royale?*"

"You bet. I got tired of *Save the World* after they started putting all the money into PvP. Figured it was time to switch over."

"What's your gamertag?"

"SammichLuva."

"For real?" Cooper and I burst out laughing.

"Yeah! A play on my name and my epic sandwich-making abilities."

"That's awesome!" I say. A girl who loves food, too.

"I'd like to take credit for it, but truthfully I used a name generator. It was so ridiculous I had to go with it." She laughs. I'm relieved that she no longer looks angry with me.

"I'm UatuxD," I tell her. Maybe Cooper will make an exception and let her join us.

"I'm Zoma44," Cooper adds. "I'd invite you to our squad but we're pretty tight."

"No problem. I've got my own," Samara says, swinging her head to the side. I watch as her tawny-coloured hair swishes behind her. I love a girl who's confident and able to hold her own.

"What squad do you belong to?" I ask.

"The one that's going to win the prize money." She smiles.

"What? The money Rick Fox is putting up?"

"I wish. Playing for Echo Fox would be pretty boss. I do compete regionally. I'm trying to head to the games though. I got to go to the *League of Legends* Championship Series last year." LCS is probably the largest eSports competition in the world. Ten teams from both North America and Europe compete. As the most-played game in the entire world the last couple of years, it'd be pretty cool to watch.

"You went to the studio in L.A.?" I ask.

"Yeah. My mom wanted to go to Disneyland. I negotiated with them to let me go to the games instead."

"Wow. Lucky," I say.

"Wait, what? You skipped Disney?" Cooper says.

"It's not what you think. My mom is dating this loser who thought that taking her and her kid to Disney would make up for the fact that he's a total perv."

"A perv? For real?" Cooper asks.

"Let's just say my mom doesn't have good taste in men."

"Wait," I say, trying to compute what she's just said. "What? I thought you said your parents are both lawyers and they want you to come and work with them someday?"

"They are," Samara says quickly.

"They're divorced then?" Cooper asks.

"They aren't together anymore," Samara admits. Why would she change the story like that? What about her parents wanting them to work all together like a big happy family? But her mother is dating someone else? Things aren't adding up, but I see Samara's bottom lip quivering, so I decide to drop it.

Cooper and I don't respond.

"I wish I could go to the games. Or any tournament circuit for that matter," I say, changing the subject back to gaming. It's pretty incredible how watching other people play video games has become this huge phenomenon. People are making a living playing video games, and the prizes are huge. Last year, Rick Fox, one of the biggest people in eSports, announced $100 million in *Fortnite* prize money, and he was scouting for the best of the best to join his team, Echo Fox. Being able to watch them in action would be pretty epic.

"It was pretty cool. Definitely the only highlight of that trip." Samara pulls her knees up to her chest and wraps her arms around her legs. Her eyes remain downcast. I want to ask her more about her family but I don't dare pry.

Rory appears from the escalator. He's carrying a few radio batteries. No one else is with him.

"No luck on the missing," he announces.

"What? You didn't find Chris?" Cooper asks.

"I checked the store but it's still locked up. He's nowhere to be found."

Chris must've rushed out through the broken entrance hoping to get to his wife after all.

"Erwin is still looking for the others."

Rory motions for George, and the two of them step outside the store to discuss something privately. I wonder what he's seen or if there are any updates.

George walks back to the group. "It looks like the storm is just ramping up," he tells everyone. "It's about to get worse." We all remain fixated on him. "I think it's safe to say that we're going to be staying here for the night. Now that it's getting dark and the storm is about to get worse, it's better for us to stay in the building until the storm subsides. Hopefully we'll have power and cell service again soon. I know being stuck here isn't easy."

Mildred starts to weep again. Peter holds her closely and rubs her back.

"We're going to die!" she says loudly. Peter shushes her. I look to Brandon and he's clenching his jaw. The last thing

I want is for him to panic again. He needs to know that we're all safe here.

"We just have to wait the storm out," I say brightly. "Think of it as a giant community sleepover!" A few people chuckle, but mostly, the group is subdued and anxious. Of all of the places I could imagine sleeping in someday, I could never have predicted the navy-blue carpet-tile floor of the Designer Dresses store, using a thousand-dollar purple satin dress as a blanket. But then Samara is here, too, and I couldn't have predicted that either, so in some ways sleeping here for the night feels like a serious upgrade to my life.

TIP #6

When she chooses you, you'll know

The night creeps by slowly and sneakily as though something is hidden up its sleeve as it descends upon us. People try to sleep but everyone seems to doze in fits and starts. Random snores are disruptive; the constant swish of dress fabric grows to be more than a minor annoyance as people try to get comfortable and stay warm. Ira wakes up hungry and wails for about an hour before Valerie can calm him and get him back to sleep. There's a steady parade to the bathroom over the course of the night. George, Rory, and Erwin take turns guiding people and I doubt any of them gets any rest.

The building continues to creak and rattle, and the rain pelts the glass roof outside the store with such force we all wonder just how much water is accumulating below us. Thunder and lightning make the air throb with power, and even though the sky is dark with night we can all sense that there is something ominous looming over us.

I've never really been scared during a storm before. While my brother, Marshall, always wants to snuggle with my parents and needs reassurance, I've always found storms fascinating. I often sit on the front step watching the clouds descend, mesmerized by their fast-moving swirl as they circle around each other like the stir of soup. I try to watch for as long as I can before my mom starts sealing up the windows and doors and directing us down to the basement. That's what it feels like now, like I'm shielded in the basement hearing the storm batter the building but unable to watch.

Once, the guys from the show *Tornado Hunters* came to our school. Two of the guys from the crew were from Saskatchewan. I couldn't believe that they'd been able to make storm chasing a career. They showed us a bunch of video clips of them tracking storms and I was mesmerized. Being witness to a weather phenomenon that even scientists can't fully predict or understand seems like a pretty cool gig if you ask me. They're often the ones to alert the authorities of a developing tornado, which means more time for people to prepare and take cover.

"My phone's dead," Cooper whispers to me.

"I still have twenty-six percent. Not that it'll matter at this rate," I say grimly. I power my phone down to conserve the battery.

Being stuck in this building in the dark is getting old fast. I am tired and hungry, and there doesn't seem to be an end in sight. "This is exhausting," I mutter.

"Yeah. It sucks," Cooper says. We both look over at Samara. She's breathing deeply and doesn't even stir at the sound of our voices.

"I think she's actually sleeping!" I say in surprise. How anyone could sleep in these circumstances is beyond me. There's nothing comfortable about it. It makes me think of homeless people and how they have to take shelter wherever they can. At least we're safe from the elements. I hope that all of the people who are homeless right now are somehow safe, too.

Samara has the navy dress draped over most of her body and her scarf is still wrapped around her like a shawl. I wish I could see her face and stare at her without her knowing — but then I realize that I'm sounding like a total creep again. I bet she looks like an angel when she's sleeping. I can only see her long ponytail splayed out like a fan across her back. Her face is tucked down toward her chest and she's curled up in a ball. The tops of her boots, on the floor beside her, have flopped down toward themselves. I spot lime green ankle socks poking out of the bottom of the dress; her legs are the colour of porcelain.

"Need help putting your eyes back in your head?" Cooper laughs but I bet he's staring, too. I quickly turn away and hop to my feet. "What are you getting upset for?" Cooper asks. I don't answer, shuffling toward the store entrance where the security guards are watching over us.

"Zach!" Cooper says louder. "Where are you going?" How can he sound so genuinely perplexed? As if he doesn't know.

"For a walk," I hiss. The last thing I want is for Samara to hear that I'm staring at her like some super sleaze. As if Cooper is one to talk. He's monopolized every moment with her even though I was the one who was showing interest in her. Now he's making it look like I'm zeroing on his girl, which I am, but I'm not. Because she isn't his girl. At least I hope not.

"Can't sleep?" George asks as I approach.

"Not really."

"Quite the storm out there," Erwin says, motioning to the glass roof.

In seconds the rain gets louder and more forceful, and we realize it's hail. It clinks against the glass so forcefully I feel the urge to duck in case it shatters.

"Is it safe to be standing here?" I ask.

"It's not the first storm this roof has handled," George reminds me. "They wouldn't use this kind of roof if it didn't hold up well."

"True," I say, though I'm not too sure. "Mind if I take a little walk?"

"As long as you're close, sure. Don't advertise it."

I chuckle. I'm glad George trusts me.

I venture two stores away. The farther I get from other humans, the eerier it all feels. There are flashes of lightning that light up the inside of the mall like quick snapshots. The light bounces off of the metal security gates that lock up the stores and then disappears just as quickly. I suddenly feel very small and vulnerable in this cavernous black building. It feels like we could be shooting a horror movie.

I rub my arms — goosebumps prickle my skin. The hail is relentless and the sound borders on ear-splitting. I stop at the railing overlooking the main floor. It is just as dark and eerie down there. I picture the water that was lapping at the door from the underground parking. Will we be leaving this building by boat? Will the water continue to rise? Just how are we going to get out of here if that happens? I think of my family again and wonder if they're safe at home. My throat closes up when I think of my mom, who's probably pacing the house in worry about me. I wish I could let them know I'm okay. I pull out my phone and turn it on, in case service has been restored in this exact instant so that I can call home, but it's wishful thinking.

A wave of loneliness washes over me. I stuff my hands in my pockets and blink back tears. I've never wanted to be with my family more than at this moment. This was supposed to be a quick storm that would strand us briefly and then we'd be sent back on our way — but things are feeling more serious as time goes on. It's been hours already. Surely the storm will subside soon. When lightning flashes again, I glance up at the glass ceiling and see masses of ice the size of softballs.

A distant rattle interrupts my thoughts. I look back toward Designer Dresses and crane my neck to see if it's coming from there but I don't see or hear anything from that direction. I wait to hear the sound again, and sure enough it's coming from a different direction. The guards have been watching over us, keeping our group contained in the store. Could it be Chris trying to find us?

I decide to walk toward the sound. I step as gingerly as I can and stay along the store gates so that I don't lose my way.

I follow the sound to the west corridor of the mall and wonder if I should go any farther. Turning the corner will put the group out of sight. But the sound is definitely closer and curiosity gets the best of me.

I make my way around the corner and freeze. Midway down the corridor I see two dark figures partly illuminated by the stream of a flashlight. They're fixated on the security gates of one store. My heart starts thumping inside my chest and my breath becomes shallow. My Spidey-senses (I wish, but a guy can dream) go on full alert. I try not to panic.

It's important to approach potential combat carefully. It can be dangerous to go alone — and running headlong into battle can be a bad idea. You must choose your battles carefully. Without weapons or a way to defend myself, I want to avoid being seen at all costs. "Hey!" a male voice booms. The flashlight turns in my direction. They've seen or heard me. I crouch down, hoping the beam of light doesn't land on me. Do I get closer to have a better look at them? Do I confront these guys? Do I turn around and let the guards handle this?

I hear footsteps. I turn back around the corner and run as fast I can back toward the group. My heart thunders in my chest. Even though I'm sprinting as fast I can, my legs feel thick and tingly, as though I'm running through quicksand. As I approach, the guards' flashlights beam down on me.

"Zach!" George calls out to me. "What's wrong?"

"There are people over there," I say, my voice strangled in ragged breaths. "They're coming. Two men!" I put my hands on my knees and try to catch my breath.

"I knew I heard something!" George says. "Get in the store, Zach!" He pushes me toward the Designer Dresses storefront and he, Rory, and Erwin brace themselves in the darkness, their flashlights and radios at the ready. The three of them walk away from the store.

"We know you're there," George bellows.

The authority in his voice wakes the people who are sleeping. They start out bleary-eyed and confused but then sense potential danger in the air and soon the group is sitting up in high alert.

I flash my phone light toward myself to let people know I'm standing there. I motion for everyone to stay where they are. I put my finger to my lips to tell them to be quiet. No one makes a sound as we strain to hear what's happening.

My desire to protect the group is overwhelming. I see all of these people who hours ago were complete strangers; now they're people I know and care about. The thought of any harm coming to them makes my stomach wrench.

The voices I hear are distant. I step back from the store into the main corridor of the mall to see if I can see anything. Flashlights are shining in all directions but there's no evidence of the men.

George emerges seconds later. "Rory and Erwin are going to look for them. Was it the guys in the track suits?"

"No. I mean, I don't think so. I think they were trying to break into a store around the corner. They were fiddling with the security gate."

"Which store?"

"I'm not sure — I don't know the rest of the mall that well."

"How far down?"

"Maybe halfway?"

"I'm willing to bet it was Spell Jewellers. That means they were trying to loot the store."

"How'd they get in? I thought the mall was empty except for us."

"Well, to the best of our knowledge. I'm guessing they came in through that door by the food court." George faces the store again. "Everyone, sorry for the disruption. Everything's okay. You can go back to sleep." He leans in to me and whispers, "We have to keep this under wraps for now. I don't want to incite any panic." I nod. Between the huge swaths of hail and the adrenaline surge from having possible intruders in the mall, everyone else's nerves must be as jangled as mine.

"I'm just going to head to the bathroom," I tell George.

"Need an escort?" George asks.

"Nah, I'm good." I laugh. I take a step away and feel a tap on my shoulder. It's Samara.

"Zach, who was there?"

"I don't know," I say honestly. I don't know how much I should say. I definitely don't want to scare her. "There were two guys trying to get into a store."

"Are you sure they were two guys?" Samara asks.

"Pretty sure," I tell her. "Why?"

"Nothing. Just wondering what all of the fuss was about," she says. "Thanks." She pats my shoulder and strolls back into the store. As much as I love to have her touch me, the friendly shoulder pat cements me safely on the friend list for sure.

I walk toward the bathrooms. A shiver comes over me. Knowing that there could be people that we don't know lurking somewhere in this dark building is pretty unsettling. I push open the men's washroom door and it creaks loudly. The first thing that hits me is the smell. It's foul and pungent. I try to hold my breath.

There is a small emergency light illuminating the room. It's brighter than the rest of the mall, which is a relief. I peer into the first stall. The toilet bowl is full. I wince and continue to the next stall. It's also full; toilet paper spills from the top of the lid toward the floor. Gross. Each stall is the same. At first, I think it must be a coincidence. I press the handle down on the next toilet but it doesn't do anything. Doesn't the city have generators to keep the water pumps going? I try the next toilet and the one after that, but no water moves through. My mind goes into overdrive. If the city is flooding like they're saying it is, they could have shut down the water system so that nothing gets contaminated from flood waters. I turn to the urinals and see that they're still empty. It probably won't be long before they're overflowing, too. I unzip my pants and pee quickly. I should've gone earlier before the washrooms got so gross.

I head to the sink to wash my hands and then remember that I can't. I take a squirt of soap anyhow and rub it into my palms. I rip off a piece of paper towel and try to wipe the excess off. Instead of feeling clean, I've made my hands feel slimy.

"Nice," I say sarcastically. Eager to get back to the group, I throw the used paper towel in the garbage bin, which is close to overflowing, too. How long can we stay in a place without proper washroom facilities? I push open the door and something brushes against my legs, making me trip. I immediately go into defensive mode and put my arms out ready to battle. Whatever it is, it's black and moving and it scurries past me. "Ahhhh!" I scream. I tear away from the bathroom door hoping it's caught in the room and not following me.

"What's wrong?!" Cooper and George try to catch their breath from running over.

"There's something in there!" I yelp. My arms are still outstretched, poised for defending myself. "It's black. It's moving."

"Did you see a spider again, Zach?!" Cooper jokes.

"Ha ha," I say sarcastically. "It was big. Like a cat maybe?"

George's eyes narrow. "An animal?"

"Yes! I tripped on it coming out of the washroom and it ran past me."

"Well, that's weird," George says. He pushes open the door without hesitation.

I back away. Whatever it was, it spooked me enough in this dark corridor. I don't need to see it again. George flashes his flashlight around as he enters the room.

"Come here, kitty kitty kitty ..." George calls out softly. "I don't think there's anything in here ..." Suddenly, he bursts out of the bathroom yelling "Run!!!" and shoves us out of the way. Cooper flies back into the wall. I fall onto the ground but scramble as quickly as I can to get up, half-crawling as I try to stand up. George trips over me and the two of us end up rolling on the ceramic tile floor.

We both race to get back on our feet.

"What's your problem?!" Cooper remains in place. He watches George and me freaking out and trying to get away from the scene as fast as we can.

"Skunk!!!" George cries. "It's a skunk!!!"

It takes a moment for Cooper to register George's words and then he hightails it toward us. He runs faster than I've ever seen him run. There's pure terror all over his face.

When we get far enough, George and I start to laugh. We laugh so hard we're in tears.

"A skunk ..." I say in between fits of laughter. "You should have seen your faces. And you were making fun of me!"

"Yeah, yeah." Cooper looks sheepish.

"I sure don't want to be sprayed. Do you?" George's whole body shakes when he laughs.

"And you thought it was a cat." Cooper shakes his head at George. "You're lucky you *didn't* get sprayed!" He clutches his stomach as he laughs.

"We've got skunks that hang around the garbage bins outside in the back. I bet one got in during the chaos of the power outage."

We get a hold of ourselves before returning to the group.

"That was a good laugh, boys," George says, wiping his eyes. "After tonight, I needed that."

"So, what? We just leave him in there?" I ask. Who's going to want to go into the washroom if they know there's a skunk in there?

"Are you going to go in there?" George challenges. Cooper and I shake our heads. *Not a chance*, I think. In a tough situation, you've got to pick your battles — and fighting a skunk will not be one of mine tonight.

"Didn't think so." He grins. "What makes you think I'm going to either?"

- - - -

It's another forty minutes before Rory and Erwin show up. Their black work boots squawk with the weight of the water they've absorbed.

"Couldn't find them," Erwin says. "We looked everywhere. The mall looks clear."

"We can't have these guys roaming the mall. Zach seems to think they were about midway down, which would put them at Spell Jewellers. We have no idea if they're dangerous or not but if they're trying to steal things during the storm, they're not exactly upstanding citizens." George is right. Those guys were up to no good.

"They might have run back out," Erwin says. "The food court entrance is only partially barricaded."

"Any way we can firm that up better?" George asks.

"With what? I think it's the best we can do."

"We'll have to keep our eyes out and remain vigilant. With any luck we scared them off for now. Maybe they've left."

"I'm not sure where they went, but the water is ankle-deep downstairs." Rory lifts one of his feet to show us. "Someone better find a way to get us out of here before they need to bring a boat in to get us."

George frowns. "The most recent reports of the storm are bad."

"What do you mean?"

"The winds have picked up. Power lines are down everywhere. Streets are blocked by broken branches. Because we're relatively safe and secure in this building, they're asking us to hold tight because there are other people who haven't been as lucky. Funnel clouds have been spotted just outside of the city, and they've been tracking a tornado along the Trans-Canada Highway. I think it's time we head back downstairs just in case."

"But what about the water?" Rory says.

"Look, staying up here in the event of a tornado is not good either."

"But what if the water continues rising?"

"I get it. I don't know what we should do." George closes his eyes and takes a deep breath. "If only I knew how long we'd be stuck in here."

"The washrooms are almost overflowing up here," I pipe up. "At least if we're downstairs we'll have new washroom facilities."

"Yeah, Zach needs a clean place to take a dump," Cooper says under his breath behind me.

"Have you been in there?" I shoot back. "How about you go and take one in there?"

Rory and Erwin laugh. "Well then, if that's what Zach needs … that decides it!"

"Yeah, does either of you have to go?" Cooper asks Rory and Erwin. They don't know about the skunk.

"There's an even bigger stink in there than before." I snicker.

"Yeah. You should go check it out. My friend Pepe is in there and he hasn't come out yet," Cooper says with a straight face.

Rory and Erwin study us, unsure if we're being real with them or not. I let out a snicker. I expect George to laugh with us but his face is expressionless. "Stop!" he says suddenly. "This is serious!"

We're immediately silent. George is visibly agitated. His face is flushed and sweat is building on his temples to the point of needing a towel to clean himself up.

"You okay, George?" Erwin asks softly.

George ignores the question. "Okay, let's get everyone up. We're moving to the other side of the mall."

TIP #7

Doing the right thing isn't always easy

"Like we're going to get a real tornado," Cooper says. I'm pushing Ira's stroller for Valerie while Ira sleeps in her arms.

"I don't know. This storm is a lot worse than anything I can remember," Erwin says.

Peter hears us talking. "The deadliest tornado on record happened in 1912," he tells us. "In Regina." Regina is about two-and-a-half hours from Saskatoon; it's the capital city of Saskatchewan.

"You mean the worst in Saskatchewan?" I ask.

"No — it was the worst tornado in Canadian history. Twenty-eight people died. My parents were in that storm."

I watch Mildred's eyes grow wide as she takes in her husband's words.

"Yeah, and there wouldn't have been any kind of warning system then, would there have been?" I say.

"Well, obviously the more time people have to respond, the better," Cooper says.

"The thing is," Peter explains, "scientists can't actually predict with certainty where or when a tornado will form. Radar can only detect when the conditions known to form tornadoes exist. It's something called ground truth. Human eyes must witness the tornado in order for it to be confirmed."

"By then isn't it too late to warn people?" Cooper asks.

"That's why warnings are often given out sooner than that. But if there are too many false alarms, people can start ignoring the warnings, thinking that the chances are pretty slim."

"Well, it's not like we get F5 tornadoes like the United States," Erwin says.

"Actually, we might get them, too," I tell him. "I remember learning about this at school. The prairies are now the northern tip of Tornado Alley. We probably get a lot more tornadoes than we know about because we have sparse population in a lot of areas and a lot of land. Some might never get spotted."

"Then why don't we have sirens to alert us like some communities do?" Erwin asks.

I shrug. "Because we rely on weather forecasts, TV, and phone alerts, I guess?"

"A lot of good that does us now," Cooper says sharply.

"Yeah, power outages make things a lot worse, that's for sure," Peter says. "How do people get the warnings if there's no power? People need lead time to get somewhere safe."

"Stop talking like that, Peter!" Mildred cries out.

"Honey, that's what we're doing right now. We're keeping safe." He wraps his arm around her shoulder and caresses her arm.

"Too bad we don't have a battery-powered radio," I say.

"Sometimes the radio posts are abandoned in emergencies," Cooper says. "Don't you get it? We're being forced to fend for ourselves. I don't even think they're trying to get to us."

"George said there were other people worse off than us that they are getting to first. I think it's like a triage system, when they sort people based on how serious their condition is and how quickly they need medical care. Right, George?" I say. George is walking at full speed, shining his flashlight around us, oblivious to our conversation. "George?"

George freezes and cocks his head to the side for a moment. We all stay quiet.

"Rory, Erwin," he whispers. They rush to his side, at the ready.

George motions with his chin toward the corridor where Spell Jewellers is. He turns to face us. "I need all of you to stay together. Come and wait over by this wall. Nobody leaves."

George nods at Cooper and me. We guide the crowd over to the wall adjacent to the elevators. It's a large open common space so there's room for us to spread out. The only seating in the area is a leather loveseat with a garbage bin at one end and a fake silk planter at the other. Immediately I park Ira's stroller against the wall for Valerie and then guide Peter and Mildred to rest on the loveseat. Cooper and Samara follow.

Peter smiles at me gratefully as he helps Mildred onto the seat of the couch. They settle in together, and Mildred rests her head on Peter's shoulder. His large hand is like a bear paw on his wife's slight shoulder.

"We should go and wake Farrah up," Mildred says. "She doesn't like storms."

Cooper and I look at Peter, stunned. Peter said earlier that they'd lost their daughter, that she'd drowned. If she had drowned, how could they go and wake her now?

Peter smiles gently at his wife.

"Farrah is resting peacefully, my love." His voice is reassuring and patient. "One should never wake a sleeping child."

Mildred nods and pats his thigh. "You're probably right, dear."

It dawns on me that Mildred is confused; she thinks that Farrah is still a young girl and that she's still alive. Cooper and I exchange a knowing glance that Peter catches and returns, confirming our suspicion.

We give Peter a sympathetic smile. He gives us a compassionate look.

"I'm sorry," Cooper says. "That must be really hard."

"There's nothing I wouldn't do for this woman right here," Peter says. "She's the best thing to have ever happened to me. When we said our vows sixty-two years ago, it was for better or for worse, in sickness and in health. Thankfully she remembers more of the good times."

"My grandma had Alzheimer's," Cooper says. "It was pretty rough on my mom."

I remember that. We were about ten years old. Cooper's mom was spending a lot of time taking his grandma to doctor's appointments or rushing over to her house when something was wrong. Cooper was the first kid in our class to get a house key and be allowed to stay home alone after school. We were all jealous because the rest of us had to either go to a friend's house where there was a parent or stay at the after-school program, which felt doubly sucky when you were the oldest kid there.

"It's definitely not easy," Peter agrees. "My girl is sure a strong one though. She's a fighter." He takes her hand and squeezes it. Mildred smiles dreamily and leans into him again.

The fact that Mildred is forgetting her life and wants to wake up the daughter who passed away decades ago feels like a blow to the gut. It's the kind of stuff in the world that feels too hard to take in sometimes.

"Where do you think George, Rory, and Erwin went?" I ask, changing the subject.

We step away from Peter and Mildred.

"Maybe they spotted those guys again."

We crane our necks to see if we can spot their flashlights, and sure enough, we see the beams bouncing across the walls at the far end of the corridor where I'd first spotted the men.

"If there are looters, what are security guards really going to do?" Cooper asks. "They don't get to carry any weapons or anything."

"They do have handcuffs," I say.

"But what if the other guys have weapons?" Samara says. I shrug.

"We don't even know if they *are* looting," I point out. "Maybe there's a perfectly legitimate reason for them to be down there." But I know it's unlikely. If you were trapped in a flooding mall, wouldn't you want to be with the majority? Don't they say there's strength in numbers?

"That's my Zach," Cooper teases. "Always believing in the best in people. I'm far too cynical."

"Me, too," Samara agrees. Great. Another thing they have in common. "Things never seem to work out that perfectly."

"I'm just saying, if it were me, I wouldn't want to be incriminated so easily."

"But that's easy; that's because *you* would never do it." Cooper's right. I've never stolen anything in my life. Well, except for Jordie Sampson's Twizzlers on a bus ride to the Batoche National Historic Site. We'd been studying the Métis people and the North-West Resistance of 1885 at school, and our teacher wanted to take us on a field trip to see the settlement along the South Saskatchewan River. It'd been a thirty-degree day, and I'd forgotten my water bottle and my spending money at home. The muffin my mom had packed for me had barely put a dent in my hunger when afternoon snack time rolled around. Jordie had bought about six packs of candy. I jokingly swiped one but Jordie didn't seem to care all that much so I just kept it and ate it. I shared with Coop, of course.

"I don't think anyone knows what they're truly capable of, especially in difficult times," Samara says. "We think we're all great people who are law-abiding and on the straight and narrow, but I think we all have a darker side."

Cooper and I ponder her words. "What are you saying?" Cooper asks, challenging her. "You're not who we think you are?"

"No, I'm not," she says matter-of-factly. "I'm just saying, when your back is against the wall, there's no telling how someone might react. They may be capable of things they would never have dreamed of doing in another circumstance."

"Like what?" I ask. I wonder just what she means by all of this.

"Well, let's see. We've already collectively broken into and taken stuff from two restaurants in the food court and a designer dress store. That alone says something. Technically we're all thieves here."

"I don't think that means we have a darker side," I argue. "It was a decision we made in order to survive. Think of it like *Boom Beach*. We are trying to build up a base and amass resources for the good of our people. We aren't intentionally breaking the law for our own benefit."

"Aren't we?" Samara says. "Whose benefit was that for then?"

"It's just different."

"Lots of really bad decisions are made in the name of survival."

"That doesn't make someone a bad person."

"In the eyes of the court it does. People steal food or write bad cheques to feed their kids. They go to jail."

"But they're not really hurting anyone. At least physically, I mean."

"A woman might think she doesn't have it in her to fight back when a man's hurting her. She may feel too weak or scared, but push her far enough and one day she might just snap and find herself stabbing him to death."

"Are you planning on stabbing someone soon?" Cooper says, laughing.

"Maybe," Samara says. "I would if I had to. And I wouldn't even think twice about it."

We wait for a smile or a laugh, but she keeps a straight face. I laugh nervously. My dream girl could be a mass murderer, and apparently, I'm okay with that.

"That's the thing," she says. "I don't think I'd lose any sleep over it."

"I hear what you're saying," I say. "But I still don't think that makes someone a bad person. I don't think you're the conscience-less, morality-depraved soul you're making yourself out to be."

"Some of us just aren't as good as you, Zachary." She says my full name and it sends tingles down my spine. She turns on her heels and heads back to the rest of the group. I watch her walk away until I can't tell where she is; I've lost her silhouette in the dark.

"Did I say something wrong?" I ask Cooper. "I think I've upset her."

"No. I just think maybe she's dealing with more than we understand," Coop says. "That, and we can't all be like Zach." He pats me on the back and smiles.

- - - -

Voices grow louder. We see light streaming toward us from the flashlights and hear the shuffling of feet.

"Check the security cameras," one of the voices says.

"Would if we could, except that's a little hard when there's a power outage." I recognize Erwin's voice.

"You're making a big mistake," another voice says.

As they approach, I see that it's the two men in the track suits. They've been handcuffed, and they look pretty irate.

"Good thing I caught these two when I did," says another voice. The man in the business suit emerges from behind George. "They would've left with half of the store."

The two men scoff. "Why don't you check his pockets?" one of them says. "He's the one who was in there stealing. You didn't find a thing on us."

The man flashes his wrist in the air. "This is a three-thousand-dollar watch. A Baume & Mercier. Why would I have any need to steal jewellery when I can clearly afford it on my own?"

"Look, I'll tell you again … we were the ones who saw him in the store. He was the one who broke in."

"A.J., don't bother. They aren't even listening to you."

"So, what? I'm going to go to jail for some other dude's crime? You're going to frame me for it? I don't think so. Joaquin, I will *not* let this happen."

"Without security-camera footage, how can I be sure?" George says. "I've got two different stories."

"And you're going to believe the rich guy over us then," the one called Joaquin mutters.

"This has nothing to do with money," George says. "It already looked bad when we walked in to see the two of you on top of him."

"We were the ones stopping him! We were trying to hold him and get him back to you guys!"

"We're not criminals," A.J. spits. "We've got wives and babies, man."

George, Erwin, and Rory exchange glances.

The business man stares smugly at the two in handcuffs. "No one in the world would believe that I would rob a jewellery store. Especially not with you two in there at the same time. Have a fun trip, boys. We'll see you in court." He laughs and walks off.

"This is unbelievable," Joaquin says. The two of them shake their heads.

"So much for doing the right thing," A.J. says.

"Look, I'm going to hold you until I get things figured out. Perhaps a jewellery store heist wasn't such a hot idea today."

Both men remain quiet, defeated.

My insides churn again thinking back to the men in the corridor. There were definitely two people. That, I am sure of. Even in the darkness it was easy to tell that there were two silhouettes.

The man in the business suit has been alone the entire time we've been stuck here. And there were definitely two people who called out to me when I spotted them. I ran back to the group scared out of my wits. Two people were coming from that very direction and they weren't acting friendly. How can it not be these two guys?

There's a sense of relief at having captured the two people I spotted. It was unsettling to know that there were people milling around the mall apart from our group. Now if we could only find Chris.

The man in the business suit raises his voice again but I can't make out what he's saying. He looks to be arguing with some of the people seated against the wall. Erwin and Rory stride over to the see what the commotion is about.

"How hard is it to get something to eat around here?" the man complains.

"How hard is it to stick around like you were supposed to?" Brandon shoots back. "Besides, you already ate."

"Well, I'm hungry again."

"We're not in the business of starving people," George says. He stomps over to the cooler and flings it open so hard the lid bounces against the wall. He takes out a taco shell and throws random fixings into the shell like he's on a speed-cooking show. He slams the lid shut and shoves the taco into the man's chest.

"You want to eat? There you are," George huffs.

The man smirks. "Are there more where these came from?" He bites into the taco.

George steps up so that the two of them are face-to-face. "What is your name, anyhow?"

"Wouldn't you like to know," the man says. He clearly has no intention of sharing his name with anyone.

"Be happy with what you get. I don't think there's any pleasing you."

"Isn't it your job to keep us all happy?" the man counters. "I'd hate for the media to hear that the mall security staff was starving us when there was food readily available."

George clenches his teeth. He scratches at his head vigorously.

"Not that you were doing your job, anyway. You couldn't keep the group together. That's not going to look so great, either."

Rory and Erwin stand in line with George. Although he's visibly seething, he's breathing deeply and maintaining control. We all take in the scene.

"Man, that guy's a jerk," I mutter to Coop. Ever since we've been stuck with him, this man has done nothing but complain or cause trouble. Any good gamer knows that in multi-player games you have to keep everybody relatively happy in order to succeed. War takes too many resources so you should always negotiate if you can. Except I don't think there's any negotiating with this guy.

Whatever George was going to say or do, he abandons it. He walks back to the cooler and slowly opens the lid. He sets his flashlight down on the lid and slowly takes out the required toppings to make two more tacos. This time his moves are calculated and deliberate. He doesn't rush, he doesn't shove the ingredients into the shells. Instead he makes them as though they're a labour of love. When he finishes, he sets the lid of the cooler back down, takes the two tacos, and waltzes past the man in the suit, who thinks they're for him. George continues walking until he gets to Joaquin and A.J., the men who are handcuffed.

"If I take off those cuffs, can I trust that you boys will stay put?"

Our eyes grow wide. George is going to take the handcuffs off of these criminals? Off of thieves who were just caught stealing?! Has he gone mad?

"You see, I'd really like to give the two of you these tacos." George turns back to the man in the suit. The man shakes his head in disgust.

"I already told you. We aren't criminals," A.J. says. "We've got nothing to run from."

"Then you'll do the right thing." George motions at Rory and Erwin to undo the handcuffs. They look as perplexed as the rest of us.

When the first cuff clicks open, the group lets out a collective gasp, as though the safety of the entire group has now been compromised.

"Are you serious?!" the suit-man bellows.

A.J. and Joaquin rub their wrists, take the tacos gingerly from George's hands, and nod at him. They don't say a word. Instead, they chew their tacos slowly.

George leaves the flashlight on the men. No one says a word. We all watch the two men eat as though lives depend on it. Who knows what they might do if we take our eyes off of them.

When the men finish, they ask George if he needs to cuff them again. A.J. even holds out his wrists for him. We wait to see what George will do.

The man in the suit shuffles up to the men and pokes Joaquin in the chest. "Of course, they need to be locked up," he spits.

"Step back," Joaquin says evenly.

"What? What are you going to do? Hit me?"

"Step back."

"C'mon then, hit me. We'll add that to your list of charges." The man pokes Joaquin again.

The air feels thick and muggy and tense. Adrenaline courses through me again as I take in the scene. Part of me wants to stand up and intervene — but I'm also scared of what might unfold.

Out of the shadows, Brandon appears behind the man in the suit. I scramble to my feet.

"No, Zach, don't." Cooper pushes me back down. What is Brandon doing?

When the man in the suit senses someone near him, he turns. "What do you want?" He's clearly amused — that is, until Brandon makes a fist, winds up, and clocks him directly in the face.

The man crumples and falls to the ground, clutching his face.

Brandon shakes out his hand; clearly, he's hurt it in the process. Some people cheer and clap. Coop and I are far too shocked to do anything but let our jaws hang open.

Is this the same guy with the panic attacks? He's up and punched someone?

The man rubs his jaw. "Oh, just you wait, you little punk!" He starts to get up.

Brandon doesn't flinch. He doesn't walk away, he doesn't look scared — in fact, he looks very pleased with himself.

George steps between the two of them and holds his arms out to his sides as if to protect Brandon.

"What are you doing?" says the man. "He's the one who hit me."

"The way I see it, you had that one coming," George says. "And this, too."

George flings out his handcuffs — likely still warm from the other man's hands — and throws them to Rory, who's behind the man in the business suit. In a swift move, he pins the man's hands behind his back before he can figure out what's happening and secures the cuffs.

"What's going on here?" the man yells. Even Joaquin and A.J. look stunned. George lifts the side of the man's suit coat and jangles the pocket. Dangling from the opening is a long diamond necklace. It must have shaken loose when Brandon punched him. George shoves his hand in the pocket and pulls out a handful of diamond jewellery.

"Let me guess ... you were framed." George shakes his head. The man is quiet.

"Nothing to say now?" George continues. "I thought you had more than enough money to buy your own jewellery."

The man clamps his mouth shut and does not respond.

A.J. and Joaquin let out a sigh of relief.

George walks up to the two of them and shakes their hands. "I'm sorry I doubted you," he says. "That was not my finest moment. I was wrong, and I apologize."

The men in the track suits nod and pat him on the back. "All's well that ends well," A.J. says.

"I'd never steal," Joaquin reiterates. "We saw him in there and thought we could take him down ourselves."

"We really were just trying to help," A.J. says.

"Well, now I'd appreciate it if you guys stuck with us, okay?"

The two of them nod.

Rory and Erwin hold the man in the suit in case he tries to run. He seems pretty docile, which makes me think he's going to run as soon as he gets the chance.

"This day just keeps getting more and more interesting," Cooper whispers to me.

I look for Samara. She's talking with Valerie and playing with Ira, who is giggling and cooing at her. I watch her face light up with joy at the baby's reaction to her. It makes me smile.

"Well, everyone ... I think we should carry on," George says. "That's enough drama for a while." The group stands and gathers their things. I offer to take Ira's stroller again. Valerie looks relieved at having the help. I think that maybe I'll be able to walk with Samara this way, but when I get the stroller turned around and the brakes off, she's walked off. My heart sinks. After a few minutes, George starts leading the way for the group. I stay close to Valerie and Ira with the stroller. Brandon falls into step with us.

"Brandon, that was awesome! I can't believe you did that!" I tell him.

He smiles wryly. "I can't believe I did it either."

"I think you spoke for all of us with that punch."

"I know it wasn't a nice thing to do, but I just couldn't take that guy anymore and I knew he wouldn't have expected something like that from me."

I smile. "Well, without it, the jewellery might not have spilled out of his pocket. I'd say you solved a crime at the same time with that one."

"That's the first time I've ever thrown a real punch," Brandon admits. "It hurt. Bad."

We both chuckle. "You're stronger than you think you are," I say.

He shakes out his hand and examines his knuckles. "You know what, Zach?" he says under his breath. "It was worth it."

Brandon has the smile of someone who has just won their first duel. Negotiations are a good start — but there are some battles worth fighting.

TIP 20

Things aren't always what they seem

"Do you hear that?" George stops in his tracks.

"Hear what?" says Rory. The group comes to a stop.

"Shhh!" George motions for the group to be quiet. I turn and look at the group of us. If it weren't for the seriousness of the situation I would have to laugh. Everyone looks bleary-eyed and dishevelled. Half are wrapped in brightly coloured party dresses, and we're all dragging our feet. We must look like some kind of zombie circus. Like a shopping episode of *The Walking Dead*.

"Who's talking?" George asks.

No one makes a sound. George turns and flashes his flashlight across the group. I look for Samara. She catches my eye quickly and gives me a smile. I can feel my cheeks getting hot. I blush and give her a little wave but then I see that Cooper is mouthing something to her at the same time; she probably wasn't looking at me at all. I quickly turn around. How can I be such an idiot? Peter points to

George, who's pressing himself up against the elevator. "What is he doing?"

George stares at the elevator doors. Another emergency light illuminates us a little better.

"Is somebody there?" he yells down at the floor, through the seam between the doors. "Can you hear me?"

We all grow silent. Sure enough, there's a soft banging noise, distant but distinct.

"Hello?!" George yells again.

"Help!" The sound is barely discernible from where we're sitting.

Cooper and I leap onto our feet and join George at the elevator.

"Someone's stuck inside. Must've been in there when the power went out," George says. "We'll get you out!" he calls back. He turns back to us. "It's funny we didn't hear the alarm."

The banging grows louder.

"Listen, try to stay calm!" George yells. "We know you're in there. We're going to get you out!"

A new adrenaline surge courses through me. "Are you hurt?" I call.

George steps away and gets back on his radio.

"We need to find something to pry open these doors," Erwin says. Rory puffs his chest out again and squares himself with the elevator door. He shakes out his arms as though preparing for a weightlifting competition and then puts his fingers through the centre slat between the two doors.

"Ladies and gentlemen, about to lift for us today is Rory — he's competing in the ninety-pound weight class," Cooper says in a deep announcer voice. I elbow him. I don't want to start laughing. Rory clenches his teeth and grunts as he pulls on the elevator doors … but nothing happens.

Cooper and I join him, getting on the ground and pulling closer to the bottom. It still doesn't move.

"We're going to have to get something." Rory steps away.

"Normally the doors can be pried open easily from the inside," George says. "If they can pull open the doors in there, they should be able to get out."

"Can you hear us?" Rory shouts.

"Yes," a distant voice replies.

"WE WANT YOU TO TRY AND PRY OPEN THE DOORS!"

"How?"

"JUST TRY WITH YOUR FINGERS!"

"We've done that!"

"WE'LL TRY FROM THIS END, TOO!"

"Zach, who do you think is in there?" Samara asks.

"I have no idea. They've probably been trapped in there for about ten hours by now though!" I glance down at my watch. It's 4:03 a.m.

"No chance of it being Chris?"

"How? The power was already out when we lost track of him. Unless the elevator runs on back-up power, I guess?"

George interjects. "The elevator is designed to go straight to the main floor if there's a break in power. It should be at ground level already."

"I can go down there," Samara offers quickly.

"Are you crazy? You need to stay up here with the group," I say, more forcefully than I mean to.

"Why should you tell me what to do?" Samara says. "You think I can't handle myself?"

"That's not what I meant," I stammer. "I just want you to be safe."

"He's right. It's up to us to handle it," George says, pointing to Rory and Erwin.

Samara crosses her arms and walks over to the railing that overlooks the ground floor. Cooper joins her. I watch as their heads lower together like they're deep in conversation. Something bubbles up inside of me — an ugly festering — a jealousy that makes my blood pressure rise to peak levels. I feel like Tobey Maguire in *Spider-Man 2*. Cooper is James Franco playing Harry Osborn. He's no longer my best friend but a double-crossing enemy dating the girl I like. Samara is my Mary Jane. And somehow, he'll justify it by saying I didn't make a move.

My neck and shoulders tighten. My veins throb with an intensity that I'm unfamiliar with. I think of *Ready Player One*. Why can't I be like Wade Watts or his avatar Parzival, fighting to save everything and then getting the girl at the end? After he wins the quest, he and Samantha move in with one another and build a future together. And she's perfect for him — into so many of the same things he is. She sees how hard he works and what a great guy he is. I think I'm invisible to Samara. All she seems to notice is Cooper.

Voices call up from down below. "WE'RE OUT! WE'RE OUT!"

Our group lets out a few cheers and some half-hearted clapping.

"Yes!" George smiles. "It worked! I better go down and check to make sure they're okay... I'll bring them up to join the rest of us."

"THIS IS CODE 70 TO GATEWAY MALL," George's radio booms. "THIS IS AN EMERGENCY ALERT. A TORNADO HAS TOUCHED DOWN. TAKE COVER IMMEDIATELY."

George presses his radio. "TEN-FOUR."

Cries of fear fill the empty space and make the hair on my arms stand up again.

"Okay," says George, "I want everyone to make their way down this stairwell here. We'll take cover downstairs. Let's get down there safely and swiftly."

"I've got the stroller," I tell Valerie. She nods gratefully. I hold open the big steel door so that everyone can make their way down the steps. I glance up at the glass ceiling as everyone makes their way past me. The hail has stopped. It has accumulated in the corners of the steel framing that holds in the glass. A soft rain makes a gentle percussion sound against the glass. The sky has gotten a bit lighter. The greenish-yellow-grey tinge of the sky confuses me. I wonder if it's the break of dawn mixing with the storm.

The two middle-schoolers, Liam and Henry, are carrying the cooler filled with our food items. I smile at them and pat the one closest to me on the back. "Thanks for helping, boys."

They don't smile back. The one I pat gives me an eye roll.

"You guys coming?" I yell to Cooper and Samara. They rush over. They're the last of the group besides Rory and Erwin. George has gone down to find the people who were stuck in the elevator.

"Thanks!" Samara and Cooper say in unison as they pass by me in the doorway. How cute. They're even talking at the same time like an old married couple.

"Whatever," I mutter under my breath.

"You first," Rory tells me, reaching for the door with his arm so that he'll be the last to go down. I push on the door harder than I should and it flings so fast it bounces back and hits Rory in the chest.

"Sorry — didn't mean that." My eyes are dark.

"You okay?" Rory asks. I don't say anything. I lift the stroller and stomp down the stairs to join the group.

Just as I'm getting to the stairwell door on the ground floor, Samara comes sprinting back in. Water sloshes up at me. She runs into the stroller and knocks me backward onto the steps.

"Oh my god, I'm so sorry!!!" She looks panicked. "Are you okay?"

"Yeah, I'm fine," I grunt. Truth is my back slammed so hard into the ceramic-tiled stairs that I'm winded and probably deeply bruised. "Are you? What are you running from?"

"Nothing," Samara says. She sits on the second-last step and stretches out her legs. "I just want to stay in here. For good."

"Are you scared?" I ask. Tornadoes sound super scary. I get it.

"Yeah. I'm scared," she says. She's turning pale.

"It's going to be okay," I say gently. I set the stroller down into the murky, ankle-deep water and try to sit up. My back feels like it's been chopped in two. I try to slide in closer to her and I can't help but wince. This is my chance to comfort her and reassure her. And where is Coop? Why isn't he clueing into the fact that Samara is not okay?

"We'll be safe." In a daring move, I take her hand. It's soft and small in mine. Even though it's dark, I move to crouch in front of her so that she knows I'm looking into her face and that I mean it. Water hits the bottoms of my pant legs and the fabric absorbs the liquid quickly like a paper towel. "I promise. We'll be safe." The darkness makes me brave and bold. I take my other hand and place it carefully on her cheek. She closes her eyes; a few tears cascade down her cheeks and slide across my fingers. Her skin feels like flower petals — so soft and silky. I brush one of her tears away with my thumb. To my surprise, Samara doesn't pull away. I wonder what she's thinking in this moment. I want so badly to lean in and kiss her.

Cooper busts through the door. Water sprays at my back. "Where are you guys?! I've been —" He makes a full-stop. I pull my hands away and jump up so quickly I can barely breathe. I don't know what to say or do so I push past Cooper and leave the stairwell. I hear the door click behind me. The two of them stay inside.

The group has crowded around George. My feet make little splashes as I join them.

"Ma'am, I think you need some medical attention," George says. His voice is calm. I peer over the other heads to see who he's talking to. It's a middle-aged woman. She has dark auburn hair that's frizzy and backcombed into a large bump on the top of her head. She's wearing a thin pink tank top with spaghetti straps and black pants that are faded in spots to a dark grey. She's got a small backpack on her shoulders and she's sitting directly on the ground in the water. The water has seeped through most of her outfit. She's frighteningly thin; her bare arms and legs are practically all bone.

"I'm fine. I'm fine," she says, waving George off. When she speaks her mouth opens just enough for me to notice that she's missing more than a couple of teeth. The remaining ones are like filed-down stubs in her mouth.

She tries to get up but then falls back down into the water. It sloshes around her.

"I've got her." A man steps forward. He's equally thin. His black T-shirt and shorts hang awkwardly off of his emaciated frame. He has shaggy dark-brown hair and a small moustache. His eyes look sunken. He grabs her wrists and we get a full view of her arms. They're bruised and show the marks of an IV drug user. He pulls her up to standing. She holds on to him for dear life.

"What are your names?"

"I'm Alec, and this is Betty." Alec is practically holding Betty up. His arms have the same tell-tale marks that hers have.

"George," Rory says. He's pointing to the floor of the elevator. A needle and an empty plastic bag are in the corner. George nods and turns to the couple.

"Are you hurt?" George asks.

"We're just fine."

George stares back and forth at the two of them. He motions for me to come to him.

"Any chance these are the people you saw upstairs?" George whispers. I shake my head no. They aren't the two I saw, and with them being stuck in the elevator this whole time, that would make it an impossibility.

"Where's my Sammy?" the woman asks, looking around.

"Who?" George asks.

"Sammy."

"There's nobody here by the name of Sammy."

The woman lets out a yelp and buries her face into Alec's shoulder. He doesn't comfort her.

"We don't need Sammy," Alec says gruffly.

"Sammy!" the woman cries.

"Are you saying that someone else is around here?" George presses. "Was there someone else with you?"

"No," Alec barks. "Does it look like someone else was with us?" Alec motions to the open elevator that is clearly empty. "We were all alone." Betty continues to cry.

The building shudders with the force of the wind and everyone freezes in fear. Even I feel myself tensing up. George switches gears. "Okay, now that we've found you guys," George motions to Alec and Betty, "we should get everyone into the stairwell. It's the safest place for us." He motions to the door. "Everyone, back into the stairwell. We've got to take cover."

He's right. The stairwell will be the safest landing spot for us.

Liam and Henry start crying. Nancy wraps her arms around their shoulders and squeezes them into herself. Rory opens the door for everyone. The emergency light outside the door brings light into the stairwell. I hang back, wanting the others to get in first. I'm also not sure if I can face Samara right now. My vantage point allows me to see her legs through the opening of the door, and I watch as her legs take her up the steps as people approach. Hanging back will give me more time to figure out how to act in this situation — this scenario where I'm crushing on this amazing girl while she's into my best friend and he almost catches me making a move on her. I don't feel as guilty as I should. I mean, I told him straight up that I was into this girl. He was so busy looking at the *Okami HD* display that he didn't pay her any attention. How was I to know that the two of them would hit it off like this?

I can't help but replay the scene in my head over and over. The feel of Samara's hand in mine, my fingertips tingling against her delicate skin. I replay the scene in my mind, the wet tears that hit my fingers as she cried. I wanted so badly to kiss her, to put my arms around her and comfort her. I wanted her to know that I'd do anything to keep her safe. In a split second, the moment disappeared, and with it, my hopes of ever getting close to this girl. Maybe some things just aren't meant to be.

TIP 84

We've been sitting in the stairwell for an hour. My back throbs even more from sitting on the hard tiles. All of our bodies perch on the steps up the winding staircase to the second floor. Wrappers, napkins, and empty water bottles litter the stairwell. We passed out as much food from the cooler as we could to keep everyone satisfied, but it's clear that we'll need more food soon if we're going to be staying much longer.

"Burritos and chips for breakfast," Liam says. It's six in the morning. "Score!"

I smile but I'm achy and tired and would do anything to go home to my own bed at the moment.

Ira is cranky and restless in Valerie's arms. She tries to nurse him but he fusses. She bounces him on her lap and sings to him softly, but he's had enough of being in the mall. Valerie looks exhausted. The batteries have died in all of our phones. The only source of light we have left are the two flashlights. Earlier the group was making small talk; now everyone but Ira sits quietly. I can't see Cooper and Samara, but I figure they're at the top of the staircase near the second-floor door. I wonder if Samara's doing okay. She was pretty shaken up earlier; I hope she's doing better. I'm sure Cooper is handling it. *Don't step where you don't belong*, I tell myself.

George is sitting in the corner of the landing between the first and second flight of stairs. It's the first time I've seen him sit since we've been in this mess. He's wiping sweat from his brow and twisting his hat in his fingers in a rhythmic motion.

"How are you doing, George?" I call up to him. He doesn't look very good, but then again we've all been looking a little worse for wear since we got stuck here.

"I'm fine." George waves me off. Ira cries out.

Valerie sighs, rummaging through her bag with her free arm. "I think he needs to be changed. I'm down to my last diaper!"

"That's no good," I say. I don't know how often babies need a diaper change but I know that no one would want to sit in a wet or dirty one no matter who they were.

"We can take care of that," George says. He waves for Erwin, who joins us. "I need you to get into the Shoppers Drug Mart downstairs," he tells Erwin.

"Now?" Erwin asks. "Isn't there a tornado about to hit?"

"We could use a few things and we might need more supplies afterward. Who knows if we'll be able to get to them after the fact."

Cooper and Samara appear from around the corner on the landing to listen in. Samara is wearing Cooper's hoodie — the hood is pulled over her head. I wonder if she's cold. I'm mad at myself. I didn't bring a hoodie; I wouldn't be able to give her one if I wanted to. A hero comes equipped with the tools he needs for every situation. Or he finds what he needs so that he can get the job done — or else he risks someone else scoring the points.

"Who has keys?" Erwin asks.

"No one," George says. Everyone is quiet.

"You want me to break in?"

"We've got to make sure we have supplies," George says.

"I doubt I'll be able to get a delivery cart."

"You could use the stroller?" Valerie says.

"Good idea!" George says. "Let's get a list going."

Erwin takes out a small notebook from his utility belt. "What do we need?"

"Bottled water, packaged food, diapers for Ira ..." George counts off of his fingers.

"What size?" Erwin asks.

"Size 4," Valerie says gratefully. "Any brand."

"Get some jars of baby food, too," George adds.

"Thank you!" Valerie says. "Here, I can give you money for them." She starts digging through her bag once more.

"No need," George assures her. "Can't even open the tills. We don't have to worry about that right now." He scratches his head. "Take all of the flashlights you see and get all of the D batteries you can. And then all of the first aid supplies you can find. There should be some kits somewhere. Add whatever gauze, tensors, and bandages you come across. Maybe some cold/hot packs. I want to be as prepared as we can be."

"I think I'll need some help with this. It won't all fit in the stroller. Maybe someone can wheel some baskets back with me?" Erwin says.

"I can!" Cooper volunteers right away.

"I'll help, too!" Samara offers.

"I can go, too," I add. It may give me some more time with Samara and allow me to intercept anything between her and Cooper.

George shakes his head. "I think two is enough. Zach, we can use you here."

Great. Once again, the dynamic duo is going to take care of things together, without me.

"Okay, let's go then," Erwin says.

I watch as Cooper shuffles down the stairs and then trails off, sloshing the stroller through the water, Samara by his side in those amazing boots.

"George, you okay?" I ask.

"I'm okay, Zach," George says, but there's a weariness to him that says otherwise.

There are a few coughs here and there, but otherwise everyone is pretty quiet. The building continues to creak and moan. We hear it through the walls, like the building is moving and stretching under the strain of the storm.

"When is this going to be over?" Valerie says to no one in particular. We all mull over her words. Being held up in the mall started as an inconvenience, but now that we've been here overnight and the storm has only ramped up — this is getting serious. When I was about eight, a huge storm ripped through the city. There were tornado warnings and numerous funnel clouds were spotted, but none actually touched down. My family camped in the basement that night. We pumped up a few air mattresses and lined them up across our family room. Marshall was terrified that night, sobbing in my mom's arms with fear of what might happen. I remember being a little scared, too, but mostly thrilled that we were breaking out of our family routine to take cover downstairs. If our parents were keeping us in the basement, things had to be serious. Emergency warnings kept flashing across the TV screen as our parents tried to distract us with a made-for-TV movie. We couldn't hear much of the storm other than the loud cracks of thunder that would penetrate the walls every so often. At times Dad would run up the stairs to take a peek outside the front window. I wanted to join him so badly but he made me stay downstairs, just in case.

"It's really coming down out there," I remember him saying. "Can't even see the Robinsons' house from the window." The Robinsons were an elderly couple who lived across the street. The rain didn't feel like a cause for concern. We'd never flooded before; the rain would always just stop and things would dry up. I'd never really given it more thought than that.

That night, I lay awake for as long as I could. I waited until I could hear the soft snores of my parents as they curled up on the air mattress beside me. I knew Marshall was fast asleep. He always slept like a rock — deeply and barely moving from the position he'd fallen asleep in. Once I was confident that everyone was sleeping, I gently rolled off of my air mattress, the vinyl crackling under my weight. I cringed until I hit the carpet, not wanting to wake anyone up. I tried to move like a ninja — smooth and stealth-like — up the stairs. I had only planned to peek at the storm but when I got to the window I couldn't tear myself away from the dazzling circus of a weather system that I knew could reduce our home to a pile of sticks. It was like watching an orchestra, with each element taking its turn in the spotlight and displaying its power in nature's perfect timing. I fell asleep in front of the window. I received a stern lecture from my parents when they found me the next morning. By then all was calm outside, as though the city were resting and healing from a relentless beating. Apart from shingles being torn off of roofs and trees snapped in half in yards and across roadways, the city had emerged relatively unscathed.

This storm feels different. There's a charge in the air, an eeriness I've never experienced before. A feeling of awe and trepidation gnaws at my stomach but it lacks the thrill I felt as that little kid. Being stuck in a stairwell in a public place away from home adds to the uncertainty. I think of my parents and Marshall again. I wonder if they're safe at home. I wonder if they slept in the basement on air mattresses again and if Marshall still needs comforting.

The bottom door of the stairwell swings open. Erwin, Cooper, and Samara wheel in the stroller and a couple of baskets of supplies, their way illuminated only by a couple of flashlights.

"George!" Erwin says breathlessly. "Shoppers Drug Mart was already broken into! Looters!"

George pales. "What?!"

"The gates were already broken open. Some of the aisles were ransacked but mostly the thieves wanted into the pharmacy."

"Of course," George says grimly. "Doesn't surprise me. No sign of them?"

"There was no sign of anyone else in the mall but us," Erwin says.

"Looking for drugs?" I ask. Everyone nods.

"Unfortunately, they can make a lot of money off of some of those medications," Erwin explains.

"So, what if it was the same people who were trying to get into Spell Jewellers?" I ask. I know I saw two people.

"It's possible they tried there, too, but got spooked after you saw them, Zach," George says. "I just want everyone to be safe. Hopefully they got what they wanted and got out of the building. I can't imagine them sticking around. We'll have to stay extra vigilant to noises and activity though, just in case."

"If they want to go back upstairs, they'll have to use the stairwell," Cooper says. I'm sure he's thinking what I'm thinking: What if these guys have weapons? What if they're dangerous?

The thought of having other people in the mall stealing stuff gives me the heebie-jeebies. I think back to Samara's comments about people doing extreme things in difficult circumstances and it makes me wonder whether or not we're truly safe in here, storm or no storm.

"Cooper, do you want to hand these out?" Erwin asks, indicating the cases of bottled water they've brought back. Cooper grabs a case and starts passing them out.

"Got everything on the list," Erwin says. "They only had two flashlights, but I got a lot of batteries." He passes them up to people for them to open. "Diapers for Ira," he says, passing some out of a box to Valerie.

"I appreciate that very much," Valerie says. She stuffs them in her bag.

"We also got him some jars of food, some Baby Mum-Mum biscuits because I know my grandbabies love them, and then we couldn't resist …" Erwin tosses her a stuffed toy with a teething ring and crinkly fabric attached to it. "Thought maybe he'd like something new to play with."

Valerie laughs. She hands it to Ira and he examines it carefully. "That was very thoughtful of you. Thank you!"

"We've got some boxes of crackers and cookies and chips here … the food in the coolers was already warm so we didn't grab anything from there," Samara says as she rummages through her basket. "And more first aid supplies in this one," she continues, pointing to the other basket.

Everybody's spirits have brightened at the goods. I feel like we've just levelled up in time for the storm. Thanks to the new flashlights and fresh batteries in the old ones, we have enough light to see by.

Cooper joins Samara once he finishes handing out the water.

"The water has risen. It's about ankle-deep all the way to Shoppers," Cooper tells us.

Samara looks down at her wet suede boots and groans. "Wish I'd picked different footwear yesterday."

"We're in the safest place we can be for now," George reiterates. He leans his head back against the wall and tries to rub some of the sweat off of his face.

Ira has settled in to his mom. He's no longer crying. Instead he's slumped against her chest, depleted. Valerie resumes her singing — she has a pretty soprano voice that carries up through the stairwell. Her lilting voice is a soothing balm for our jangled nerves.

I study the faces of the people around me in the dim light. They are lost in thought; perhaps they're contemplating the gravity of the situation as well. George has been our compass on this journey so far, working to keep everyone together and safe. The weight of the responsibility is etched on his face.

"George?" I say. George's hat tumbles down the steps. His arms go limp for a second before the rest of his body slumps forward. "George!!!" I shriek. I race up toward him and hold his head up with my hands.

The panic in my voice seems to snap everyone back into high alert. "George?!" I shake him by the shoulder and try calling his name into both of his ears but he doesn't move. "Help!" I yell. But I know that there will not be medical assistance on the way at this point. We're on our own. Rory steps behind George to help while Erwin slides in beside me. The flashlight beams all swing toward us.

"I think he's unconscious!" I say. "Let's lay him down."

Erwin loops his arms through George's from under his armpits and the three of us gently lower him onto the landing.

"Check if he's breathing," Rory says.

Erwin lowers his face down to George's to feel for any air. We study his chest for movement but see nothing.

Rory checks for a pulse.

"I've got nothing," he says. The three of us look at each other with horror.

"I think he's having a heart attack," Erwin says. "Go get the defibrillator and the first aid kit."

Rory leaps to his feet and runs down the stairs to the main level as Erwin straddles George's abdomen. "Zach, do you know CPR?"

"Yeah. I'm training to be a lifeguard."

"Okay, I'm going to need you to take turns with me."

I nod. I know CPR but I've only ever practised on a dummy. I'm about to perform CPR on a human in a real-life situation. This is no simulation. I wish I could give him a chug jug, a shield potion, or some slurp juice to magically heal him, just like in *Fortnite: Save the World*, but real life isn't that easy. I take a deep breath and watch intently.

He's counting under his breath as he does chest compressions.

"Zach, I'm going to do ten more compressions and two more rescue breaths and then you're going to take over."

"Okay," I say. My insides tighten so hard I wonder if I'm going to pass out. I can't freeze in fear now. I have to do this right. I watch as he finishes and I place my hands together and loop my fingers in order to take over. Erwin nods at me.

I line up my hands with George's chest and push down on his sternum. I count out my chest compressions. Erwin's talking into his radio. "We have a medical emergency here," he says. "I've got a man in his fifties, unconscious, not breathing. Suspected heart attack."

"Erwin," I say, shaky. "It's almost time for you to take over." All my training has come rushing back to me; I know it's important to switch out regularly so neither of us gets too tired.

He nods. "You're doing great, Zach."

"Okay, last compressions," I say. I continue with my rescue breathing and then Erwin takes over. Sweat beads on Erwin's forehead. He's wheezing with the work. I realize that I've been holding my own breath, and when I release it my stomach unclenches just a bit.

Rory bursts back through the door with a first aid kit and the defibrillator. Flashlights swivel toward him and we shout for them to turn back to us so we can see what we're doing. He scrambles up the steps to us. Rory unpacks the defibrillator and starts setting it up.

"Can you unbutton his shirt?" Rory asks. I reach for George's shirt and try to unbutton it but my fingers fumble with the adrenaline surging through me. "It's okay, just rip it."

I tear open George's shirt. A few buttons fly off and roll down the steps behind us. His chest hair is dotted with grey; his skin looks pallid.

"We're going to have to shave him," Rory says. He reaches for the razor in the kit and runs it across George's chest in short, quick strokes. I can see that he's shaking. His clumsy fingers remove the stickers from the defibrillator pads and place them on George's chest.

"We're ready. Move back."

The machine instructs us to move away as well. It beeps loudly and the first shock is delivered. George's body jerks upright with the force of the charge.

Erwin resumes the chest compressions. I watch helplessly; George still seems lifeless.

"Zach," Erwin says. I take over again.

"Good job," he says. My arms are sore from the strain. I feel sweat slide down my back in a persistent stream as I continue the compressions.

Come on, I think, as I keep up the steady rhythm on his chest.

George's body suddenly tightens and he takes a large gasp of air. His eyes open. I take my hands off and we all watch as George sputters back to life.

"Oh, thank god!" Erwin shakes George with his hands. "You scared me there, buddy."

"What happened?" George tries to move but winces.

"Don't move. Just rest. We think you had a heart attack."

George groans. "I ..." He drops his head back onto the landing.

"It's okay. Just rest," I say. I feel such incredible relief at seeing him with his eyes open.

George reaches out to me. I squeeze his clammy hand.

The rest of the group erupts in cheers. I look around at them. I was so immersed in trying to save George that I completely forgot everyone around us. Erwin pats me on the back.

"You did great, Zach."

"Thanks; you, too," I manage. My lips tremble; my throat is thick with emotion. It takes me a moment to realize that I'm crying.

The rest of the people higher up in the stairwell are all looking down on us. In the semi-darkness, I can make out Cooper and Samara at the top of the crowd. Pretty sure they're both grinning down at me.

"Couldn't have done it without you," Erwin says. I nod, but the tears fall so fast they blur my vision.

"It hurts," George whispers.

"We know," Erwin assures him. "You just had the scare of your life. Now we have to wait for medical attention."

"Why? I've got you guys," George croaks.

We all smile ruefully. It's just sinking in that we've saved his life — and I've had a hand in it. The thought is almost more than I can process. Of all the things a person could grow up to be, I've always wanted to become a doctor. The closer I've come to picking a career path, the less sure I've been — until possibly now. All of a sudden, the idea of me as a doctor doesn't seem as crazy. Being able to gain the skills to help someone when they're hurt or sick — it feels like an amazing privilege.

But George isn't out of the woods yet. His eyes flutter between open and closed. He's clearly very weak.

"Is there an ambulance on the way?" I whisper to Rory.

He shrugs. "They said they'd get here when they could. Who knows when that will be."

"What do we do until then?"

"Just keep him as still and as comfortable as we can."

My stomach clenches again. George has to be okay.

I back away from George and make my way down to ground level. I take the empty spot on the bottom step and hold my head in my hands. Cool tears slide down my cheeks. Surges of both gratitude and loneliness make me cry harder. I don't know what to do with all of these emotions. I'd do anything to be home right now in the safety of my own bedroom. I'd do anything to hear my parents chatting while making breakfast, the familiar clinks of the dishes as one of them sets the table.

Maybe more than that, I wish for my mom. I wish for her arms around me just like how she held Marshall, calming him during the storm. Maybe I'm not as strong as I think I am.

A warm hand rubs my forearm. Samara. She's come to check on me. I don't know if I want to look up. I don't want her to see me like this — crying and freaking out like a scared loser. I quickly wipe my face as best I can with my fingers before looking up.

"Zach?" But it's not Samara. It's Valerie. Part of me is relieved that it's not Samara after all. I glance up at her, her long brown hair framing her face. In this moment she reminds me of my mom. Maybe at this moment any mother is enough. She sits down beside me.

"Come here," she says gently.

She pulls me to her for a hug. Instead of feeling embarrassed or awkward, I squeeze her tight. Choking sobs erupt from me. She holds me close and rubs my back.

"It's okay, sweetie," she says softly. For a moment I imagine she really is my mom. I draw as much comfort from her as I can, my body shuddering. "You did an amazing thing, Zach. I'm so proud of you."

"Thanks," I whisper. I can feel snot running down my face from crying so hard.

"Seriously. That was amazing. You saved George's life." She continues to hold me until I start to regain my composure. "Are you okay?"

I nod. She hands me tissues from her purse and I use them to dry my face and blow my nose. My head is pounding from crying so much; my eyes feel puffy and swollen.

"George is going to be okay," Valerie assures me.

"I hope so." I sniffle.

"You looked like you needed a hug."

"I did." I look up the stairwell but I only see Nancy — who's holding Ira for Valerie — Rory, Erwin, and George, plus the others who have resumed their same spots in the stairwell from before George fell over. I'm grateful that it's dark and that Samara hasn't seen me cry like this. Whatever kind of hero I might have looked like when I was doing CPR on George has disappeared; now I look like a total wimp.

TIP #10

"Stay away from me!" a girl's voice screams from higher up. Our heads all snap up to try to figure out what's going on. "Get away!"

Rory scrambles up the steps. Although I'd rather run up the stairs behind Rory, instead I take his place beside George, who seems to be sleeping.

"I mean it!!" The scream gets louder. I wonder if the young woman's voice could belong to Samara. Curiosity gets the best of me.

"I gotta go see," I tell Erwin. He nods and hands me his flashlight, but he doesn't look impressed that I'm leaving.

"What's going on?" I hear Rory ask. I get up to the top of the stairwell near the entrance to the second floor. It *is* Samara screaming. She has backed herself into the corner. She's still wearing Cooper's hoodie, but the hood has been pulled off. She looks panicked. Cooper's frozen in the middle of the staircase.

"Get these people away from me!" Samara yells. I shine the light up toward her and realize she's referring to the two people from the elevator, Alec and Betty. They're hovering near her, looking strange and menacing.

"Sammy!" the woman cries out. She reaches toward her but Samara flinches.

"No!" Samara yells.

"You're Sammy?" Rory asks.

"MY NAME IS S-A-M-A-R-A." She enunciates each letter carefully.

"Sammy, please," Betty pleads.

I quickly step past everyone to get to Samara; I approach her with my hands out in front of me.

"No," she says to me, too, shrinking back against the wall.

I feel a sharp sting.

"Please, leave me alone," Samara cries.

"Ma'am, I need you to step back, please," Rory says to the woman.

"I don't have to step back. She's my daughter."

My jaw flops open. The woman from the elevator is Samara's mom? Why didn't she say anything?

"Just grab her already or I will," Alec says gruffly.

"You will not *touch* me." Samara's words are like daggers. She slides down the wall to the ground, sobbing.

"Can you get them away from her?" I ask Rory. I can't stand seeing Samara so upset.

"Just grab her and let's go," Alec says again to Betty.

"Sammy. Please. You need to come with us."

"Ma'am, you can't go anywhere right now. This is the safest place for us at the moment."

"You can't tell us what to do," Alec spits. "She's coming with us."

He steps forward, grabs the front of Samara's T-shirt with his fist, and pulls Samara up to standing.

"NO!" she screams. She pummels him but he drags her to the door in one motion.

"You go," Rory roars, "but the girl stays here." He grabs Samara by the shoulders and jerks her away from Alec. I'm impressed. When I first saw his lanky frame, I thought a slight breeze could blow him over. But he isn't backing down from Alec at all.

"Good riddance then," Alec spits. He gives Samara an angry shove and Rory catches her before she falls. Alec leaves the stairwell, and Betty rushes after him.

"Do we let them go?" I ask. Rory nods.

"I can't keep anyone here against their will. In an ideal world, everyone would stick together and listen to my advice, but people rarely do." Rory continues down the stairs back toward George and Erwin.

I reach out for Samara but she shoves me away and barrels down the stairs past me into the darkness below. It feels like a punch to the gut. I don't know what to do. I start to follow her but Cooper puts his arm in front of me.

"Just let her go," he says. I hear her splash into the water below and out the stairwell door.

I look at him, puzzled. "Are *you* going to go?" I ask him. Can't he see how much she's hurting?

"Do you want me to?" Cooper asks. What kind of question is that? What kind of guy doesn't comfort his girl when she's upset? I bat Cooper's arm away.

"What is your problem, Zach?" Cooper's voice rises.

"What's my problem? You know what my problem is." I try to keep my voice down but I know the people around us are listening.

"No, I don't!" Cooper shoots back. His dark hair flops in front of his eyes. He shoves it behind his ear and studies me.

"You went right after her even though you knew that I liked her," I say.

"I went after Samara?" Cooper says, incredulous.

"Don't play stupid. You've been with her since this all happened."

"Are you kidding me right now?" Cooper's eyebrows knit together. My flashlight shines up at him, casting murky shadows across his face.

"You've practically been following her around like a puppy dog. Panting after her. At least try to make it a little less obvious. Plus, she's wearing your clothes now. How do you explain that?"

Cooper seethes. "Take it back, Zach."

"Take what back?"

"Do you really think I'd try to steal your girl from you?"

I remain silent.

"Do you?!" Cooper's voice rises. "You tell me you've met the girl of your dreams. Then you spend most of your time with other people and you're going to get mad at me?"

"Well, it worked out for you, didn't it? Gave you the perfect opportunity to swoop in."

"You're kidding. Unbelievable, Zach." Cooper shakes his head vehemently.

"You're going to say you haven't?" I challenge him.

"I figure if you met someone that special, that you're going gaga over, I had to check her out. Make sure she was good enough for you. And you know what?!" Cooper yells. "She's great. She's everything you hoped she'd be. But here's the thing, now I'm not sure if you're good enough for her." Cooper turns on his heels and storms up the stairs, headed for the same door that Alec and Betty exited from.

Cooper's words stab me raw. I reel from what he says. How could I have misinterpreted things so badly?

I go after him. Luckily, I'm faster and I throw my body in front of him before he can reach the top.

"I'm sorry!"

"Sorry isn't good enough, Zach. Not this time."

"Coop, I'm serious. I messed up. With you, with her …"

"Yeah, you did."

"You guys just looked so cozy with each other —"

"Don't!" Cooper cuts me off. "What kind of friend do you think I am?"

"The best. My best friend."

"Maybe," Cooper says. "Or at least I thought so."

"She doesn't want me anyhow. I think she likes you more."

"Oh God, Zach. How blind can you be?"

This time I really don't understand. Samara has barely shown an interest in me. Am I this bad at reading people?

"She didn't want me a few minutes ago."

"Why do you think she wants to get away? She's embarrassed. And the hoodie — it was to try to disguise her. She had a feeling her mom was still in the mall and she was worried that she was the one stuck in the elevator. She didn't want you to know the truth. Clearly the woman wasn't at home cooking a turkey dinner."

"Who cares about that?" My frustration mounts.

"We're not all blessed with a perfect family life like you, Zach," Cooper points out. "Even me. You know that. My parents don't have time for me so they make up for it by throwing money at me to keep me happy. Your family is the closest thing I know to perfect. You guys are like a freakin' sitcom. Complete with laugh track and the cheesy hugs to make everything better. The rest of us might feel a little jealous and might not want to share our less-than-stellar family legacies."

I think of Cooper's parents, his home, his room, how he gets anything he wants. He's right. His parents are rarely home. They don't have dinner together. They rarely check in to see where Cooper is. He can practically do whatever he wants and they don't even realize he's gone. I've spent a lot of time being jealous of him and everything he has, but maybe I've always been the lucky one. Guilt and regret creep over me.

"Coop — I know I messed up."

"Big time." Cooper shakes his head at me. Other than spats over food or games, we've never really fought much. Our biggest fights up until this point have been over trolling each other, stealing kills playing *Fortnite*, or taking out the Nexus in *League of Legends* and bragging about it. Hardly material for serious friendship wars.

Cooper turns his back to me and stomps up the stairs.

"Where's he going?" Rory asks as the steel door slams behind Cooper.

"Just give him a few minutes," I say. "Just let him cool off."

No one says anything. There's no way they didn't hear our conversation.

I want to follow Cooper and keep apologizing, but I know better. He needs some time. I get it. I messed up huge. How would I feel if Cooper was accusing me of the same thing? I'd never do that to him — not for any girl — and yet I made myself believe that he'd do it to me. What is wrong with me?

TIP #11

Admit when you're wrong, apologize, and learn from your mistakes

After what feels like hours, I decide to see if I can make things better with Cooper.

"I'll be right back," I tell Rory. I push open the steel door and step out onto the second floor. I cast the flashlight beam around in the dim light, hoping to spot Cooper. I feel terrible. I immediately start thinking of how I can make things better between us, patch things up since I can't erase what happened. How can I make things up to him? How can I show him how sorry I am?

He's nowhere to be seen. I want to find him so we can talk it out more, even though I know that's not what he wants right now and I risk him rejecting me. There's so much going on — and so much uncertainty as we sit holed up in this building. I feel like we need each other more than ever right now; instead I've gone and messed things up. Now he doesn't want to talk to me. I get it. I deserve it. But we're also going through one of the scariest times of our lives and if there's any time we could use each other for support, this would be it.

I hover on the second floor, just outside the stairwell door under the emergency light. Being alone in this moment makes my body shiver; pangs of regret and lonesomeness prick at me. It feels like me against the world. I'm illuminated by this little light in a sea of darkness. Like a theatre production where I'm the solo actor — the person in the spotlight on display for all the world to see. I picture myself on a stage. Everyone is watching. I lead into my monologue — a pathetic tale of self-pity in which no one feels any empathy or concern for my plight. Rather, the crowd turns on me. I duck as things are thrown my way. I try to explain myself but the jeers get louder until I'm forced to run off the stage for my safety.

This whole situation feels surreal. Like we're part of the real-life version of a virtual reality life-simulation *Sims* game, and someone is controlling our characters like a great big social experiment. Except this is one I don't want any part of.

I don't want to go back to the group and have to put on a brave face again. Samara and Cooper are off working out their own hurts, each of them alone somewhere in the darkness. I guess it's time for me to work out mine. I'm like Wreck-It Ralph, seen as the bad guy when I only want to be the good guy in it all.

"It was a mistake," I whisper to myself. I rub my arms to try to get rid of the goosebumps and decide to step away from the light. That way, no one will see the tears that are forming all over again.

TIP #12

Earn her trust

After taking time to try to make sense of what I've done, the need to find Cooper and Samara and try to make amends gnaws at me so much I start pacing; in the meantime, the storm has only intensified and I start to feel that regardless of whether or not they accept my apologies, I need to find them and bring them back to the stairwell so that I know that they'll be safe. It's not about me anymore. I mean, of course I want to restore our friendship, but ultimately, I care more about their physical safety in the midst of this crazy storm.

Since I know that Coop is upstairs somewhere, I decide to look for Samara. I carefully step through the maze of legs as I make my way to the first floor.

"Rory," I tell him when I make it to the landing. I shine my light at George, who's still lying on the landing next to Rory. Someone has given him a jacket or something to use as a pillow; another jacket is draped over him as a blanket. "I'm going to get Samara."

"We'll send Erwin —"

"No. It's gotta be me."

Rory nods. He must've heard the argument between me and Cooper. I'm pretty sure everyone did. He doesn't look too happy about me going but he doesn't try to stop me either.

"Be quick," he says. He's breathing heavily and looks exhausted. "I need you back in this stairwell."

I nod and pick up my pace. I've got to find her. I've got to talk to her and see if she's okay. I get to the bottom and push open the door, shoving a big wave of water aside, and I shine the flashlight across the mall floor. She shouldn't be out here. She should be in the stairwell with the rest of us where she's safer.

I slosh through the water and shine the light as quickly as I can in all directions hoping for a glance of her. It dawns on me that if she really doesn't want to talk to me she might see me coming and deliberately move to stay away from the light.

"Samara?" I call out gently. "Sam?"

I hear nothing but the whistling of the wind from the storm above and the splashing water from my steps. I keep walking, hoping I'll come upon her. The silvery security gates that protect the stores flash eerily in the light. Would she have really gone far knowing that the storm was so bad and with the mall so dark?

"Sam?" I call out again. And then I see her. She's on a bench, bent forward with her head resting on her knees and her arms around her shins. She doesn't move or acknowledge me. I tiptoe closer but the sound of the water gives me away.

"Are you okay?" I ask. She's shaking. I place my hand on her arm as gingerly as I can. When our skin touches, she flinches and tucks into herself even more.

"I'm sorry," I say quickly. I don't want to do anything that would make her more upset. Her body is racked with silent sobs until an animal-like sound erupts from her when she finally takes a deep breath. It breaks my heart. I sit down beside her.

"What can I do?" I ask helplessly.

"You can't fix everything," she says through her tears. "Not everything is a problem for you to solve, Zach."

Immediately I feel terrible. I didn't mean to upset her. I just want to help. "I just hate to see you like this," I say. "You don't deserve this."

"Deserve what, Zach? Tears? Being alone in a building where help isn't coming?"

She looks up at me. Her mascara has run down her face in thin black lines.

"Help will come," I say dumbly, but I regret the words as soon as I say them. This is not what she needs right now; these placating words mean nothing.

"Or do you mean the fact that my dad is actually dead? That he died five years ago? Or do you mean my mother, who's a drug addict? Or her creepy boyfriend who keeps her high? Or how her boyfriend is mean and violent to both of us? What is it that I don't deserve?"

I'm frozen in place. I don't say a word.

"And then he wants to take me back home with them when I've finally found a way to escape."

Samara is crying so hard I worry she's going to pass out. I want to hold her and wipe her tears but I don't dare touch her. It's the first time in my life that I have no idea what to do.

"I'm sorry," I whisper. "I'm so sorry this has happened to you."

My insides grow hot with rage. I want to find that Alec dude and beat him. I want him to see the damage he's done and then suffer for it. A kid should never have to worry about this kind of thing — not ever. But I don't know what to do in a situation like this.

"Have you told anyone?" I ask.

Samara shakes her head. "Not until today."

I nod. Samara wipes her face with her hands.

"When you said you spotted those people in the mall, and then we heard that people were stuck in the elevator, I knew it was them and I didn't want them to find me. I explained to Cooper that things weren't so hot at home so that he'd understand why I was acting so strangely and trying to hide."

I think back to Cooper and Samara standing away from the crowd when we heard people in the elevator. I thought they were trying to steal time together when really, she was confiding in him a horrendous secret. The thought makes me ill. I'm such a jerk.

"I think you need to tell the authorities," I say. "He deserves to be in jail."

Samara nods. "Except then they'll probably send me to foster care. My mom will follow that loser. She's already chosen him over me."

"She doesn't know what she's doing when she's high," I say. The truth is, I know nothing about drugs and addiction and how they make people act.

"She's not high *all* the time," Samara says. "And she still chooses him."

"That's why he needs to be out of the picture."

"The court will make my mom go to rehab." She tightens her ponytail and wipes her face again.

"Isn't that a good thing?"

"Not if I get put into foster care," Samara cries. I see how tricky this is — how doing the right thing isn't always so easy.

"I'm so sorry," I say again. This time Samara softens and leans toward me. I pull her in for a hug. My heart pounds so quickly and loudly I wonder if she can feel it against her.

She puts her head against my shoulder and I smell her coconut and honey shampoo again. My stomach does a million little flops.

"She wasn't always this kind of mom," Samara says. She's sniffling and hiccupping. "Once upon a time she baked cookies and read me stories and acted like a real mom."

My mind flashes again to my mom and how fortunate I am.

"My dad died when I was eleven, and it all went downhill from there. I could barely get my mom out of bed for months and then when I did, she started staying out late and hanging out with partiers. Without my parents, the law firm fell apart. All it took was a couple of years and she's turned into a completely different person."

I squeeze her against me like Peter squeezes Mildred to assure her she's safe. Samara seems to relax into me a bit.

"Then I'm sure you'll get her back," I say.

"If she doesn't kill herself first." Samara's voice turns bitter. "I'm so angry at her. For making me lose two parents. Even if she wasn't the one who died, I still lost her. And then Alec …" Samara chokes on her words and begins to sob again.

I can't imagine what this girl has been through and how broken she must feel inside.

"If I find that guy …" I start. My fists clench — an automatic response.

"It's not your battle to fight," Samara tells me through her tears.

"But I care about you. And no one should have to go through that. He deserves to be punished for the things he's done," I say through clenched teeth. "Look … whatever it takes, I will help you. I'll be there for you in any way that I can."

"Zach, we hardly know each other," Samara says, sighing.

"What do you mean? Hasn't the last day felt more like a lifetime? We've already slept under the same roof, had our meals together … it's like we're roomies."

Samara lets out a little laugh. The sound makes my soul dance. I love to see this girl smiling and happy.

"I guess," she says. "It definitely feels like we've known each other for far longer."

"Nothing like a natural disaster to bring two people together," I say, but then stop quickly. No one has said anything about the two of us becoming a couple. "Sorry. I mean, as friends. You know," I stammer.

Samara nods and pulls away from me. Even in the dim light from my flashlight down at my side, I can see she looks upset. I immediately regret my words. There's no way she wants to be a couple. I'm dreaming.

"But seriously, I'll be there for you. Through this. Through whatever. That's what friends are for," I add for good measure.

Samara stands up and brushes off her skirt. "We should get back."

I look for the emergency light by the steel door and beat her to it. I pull the door open for her.

"Thank you," she says quietly. Under the emergency light, her face looks sad. I follow her in and watch as she bounds up the stairs into the darkness, most likely to be as alone as she can in these circumstances. But I have to follow her up. Cooper is still missing and it's time to make things right with him, too.

TIP #13

There's always a rainbow
after every storm

I've lost track of Samara by the time I reach the top, but I leave her to whatever quiet spot she's found in the darkness and I press on. I need to find Cooper. The metal door clicks shut behind me. A distinct rumbling sound fills the air and makes the hair on my skin stand up. I've got to find Cooper before this storm goes full intensity on us. I spin around. My flashlight illuminates a figure. It's Cooper. I'm hoping he'll head back into the stairwell with me now that he's had some time away. Cooper's a pretty level-headed, easy-going guy; he's not one to get angry generally. I've never seen him as angry as this, except when Josh Logan's name comes up. Cooper knows what Josh Logan is capable of, and to say he's not a fan of the guy would be an understatement. He's about the only thing I've seen Cooper lose his temper over. Knowing that Cooper is just as angry with me right now really sucks.

We've always had a really solid friendship. The kind that feels worn-in and comfortable. He's been my best friend for so many years I can't even remember how it all started. I was an idiot to accuse him of wanting Samara.

"Coop!" My voice cracks with emotion.

He doesn't respond or acknowledge me. Instead, he ducks behind me and pushes open the stairwell door. Even if it's not the time to make things right with him, I am flooded with relief. I want to get back to the safety of the stairwell, considering how loud this storm sounds. I follow him in.

"Get in here!" Rory says when he sees us.

A high-pitched whistling sound echoes from a distance. "What's that?" I ask, of no one in particular. We all concentrate on the noise. At first it sounds like a train barrelling down tracks but then the sound builds. It grows louder and closer. "Boys, we need to head down. NOW." Rory pulls Cooper and me down the stairs, closer to the where rest of the group is huddled.

We all move lower, pressing closer to each other. The people in the first staircase squish in to make room for those of us moving down from above. The smells of our unwashed bodies and our fear meld together.

The sound becomes a gigantic roar — like a wild animal, hungry and unleashed. It becomes so deafening that we have to cover our ears. The walls start to shake. The noise makes my chest pound.

"Take cover!" someone yells, but it's faint against the clatter above us. My ears pop as a sound like a CF-18 jet

screams over our heads. We all crouch down with our
arms over our heads as the wind hammers the building. The screech of twisted metal sends shivers down my
spine. The stairwell door upstairs bursts open and bangs
loudly against the wall above. From my vantage point near
the top of the lower staircase, I can see the glass ceiling
through the upper doorway. There's a big jagged hole in
the roof, the sky above framed by pointy shards of glass. I
catch a glimpse of dim daylight: a slate-coloured sky that
churns like a washing machine drum and flashes shades
of an eerie light green.

I think I see other things flying about through the
second floor, maybe glass or building materials but I
can't be sure and I don't want to keep looking. *It's the
tornado*, I realize. *It's blowing this place apart before
my eyes.* I squeeze my eyes shut and fling myself over
Cooper, terrified that something might happen to him.
I'm disoriented, as though the world has been turned on
its axis. The steel door above flaps back and forth wildly,
and I look one more time to see a rainbow of things
swirling in the air. I grip Cooper and the stair rail with
all of my might. We could be the next thing sucked up
into the barrelling cell.

Showers of glass and metal zip through the air; the
metal snaps like toothpicks and careens into the swirl of
darkness. I can no longer hear any of the people around
us in the blare of the tornado; instead I say a silent prayer
for all of them — hoping that everyone will stay sheltered
from this annihilating storm.

Then, in a move of unimaginable force, the steel door is torn from its hinges and disappears into the swirling vortex. There is nothing but a flight of stairs between us and the mouth of this pressurized monster. The possibility of death dances around me like I've come upon the final boss, an evil lord haunting me. There's no thrill to be had here — only a terror that seizes me and leaves me breathless.

A piece of metal comes flying at me from the second floor, just missing my head. The roof has been blown clear, leaving us exposed to the storm's relentless beating. If it weren't for George making us take refuge here in the stairwell, we might have been sucked up like ragdolls. I realize I don't even know where he is; he's got to be lower down on the stairs somewhere with the others. I just hope that he's still with us.

I'm caught between not wanting to see what's happening and not being able to tear my eyes off of what's unfolding before me. Being in the mouth of this beast and knowing that I'm at the mercy of its grip — an iron-clad fist that I have no choice but to surrender to — makes me feel infinitely small and vulnerable. This is how humans come to understand that they are no match for Mother Nature. Stunning and exacting in her abilities, her force is formidable.

I glance down the stairwell. Heads are bowed and arms clutch the handrail; this metal piece feels like the only thing keeping us from being sucked into the dark abyss above us. If the roof can blow off, then surely the screws keeping the handrail in place barely stand a chance. My back is seizing from hanging on so tight. The wind is so strong it makes the skin on my face flap. To distract myself I think of how my dog, Jasper, loves to stick his head out of the car window and feel his jowls flap in the wind. I want to cover my ears but I don't dare move my hands. Instead I try to go deep within myself to a place where everything feels quiet and peaceful. That place where a voice tells me that it will all be okay. I squeeze my eyes shut and try to concentrate, but all I can think about is whether or not I'm going to be swept away. The air is literally screaming around us. Tears prick my eyelids as my arms throb from holding on so tight.

And then — like a vacuum is switched off — everything that was being sucked and tossed comes crashing down. It rains down to the ground like a mixed salad of debris. Wood and metal and glass pelt the stairs above me and bounce toward me. I tense up to brace for the impact but most things narrowly miss me. A long shard of glass makes a straight shot down the stairs and bounces off the wall, slicing me across the arm. I feel a sharp sting.

In mere seconds, the deafening sound has passed, though we can still hear it as it moves away from us, the tornado carrying on its path. Slowly, we start to sit up and gather ourselves again. Almost everyone is either crying or sitting in a state of shock. The air is thick and muggy; despite the open door above letting in the early dawn light, it's hard to see through the particles that swim around us.

"Everybody okay?" Erwin calls out. No one really answers. I wonder how George is.

"Coop?" I ask. I move off of him to give him some space.

He sits up and brushes himself off. He gives me a slight grin to let me know he's okay. "Well, that was something," he says. Maybe someday this will make for a pretty epic story, but right now we're just shell-shocked.

I can't go another minute without making things right with him.

"Coop, I'm the biggest jerk. Honestly. I'm so sorry," I start.

"It's fine," Cooper assures me. "It's done with."

"No, it's not. I should never have accused you of trying to get with Samara. I was totally out of line. And then this tornado …" My throat closes up and I can't get my words out. "I can't imagine something happening to you."

Cooper nods. "I know. You threw yourself over me. I could barely breathe."

"I won't ever let a girl come between us," I say pointedly.

"Deal."

"No, seriously. I mean it! The bro code all the way."

Cooper nods. He holds out his hand and we fist bump. Then he gasps. "Zach! You're bleeding!"

I look at my arm where I felt the glass hit, and sure enough I have a large gash. Blood is dripping down my arm.

"I'm fine," I say, but I feel a little woozy when I see the cut for myself.

"That doesn't look fine." He calls down for the first aid kit and it slowly gets passed up to him.

"You guys need a hand?" Erwin asks.

"No, we're good," Cooper says. He looks for a roll of gauze and the scissors.

"Your turn to play doctor," I say. My voice is shaky and small. I almost don't recognize it.

"This looks pretty bad, Zach." Cooper grabs the flashlight from me and inspects my arm closely. "You're going to need stitches."

"Just wrap it. It'll be fine," I say. There are far more important things needing attention than my arm. "We've got to make sure everyone is okay. George, Samara, Peter, Mildred, Valerie, Ira ..." I pause. I don't want Cooper to think I'm leaving to play hero again.

"Okay. Let me get this wrapped and then we'll check on everyone." He looks me in the eye. "Together."

I nod. This is why Cooper is my best friend.

I watch him wrap my arm carefully. He secures the gauze and then places the remaining items back into the first aid kit. My arm throbs but I can't think about it right now. I have to know if everyone is okay.

"Let's go!" I say.

Cooper helps me up.

Now that the door has been ripped off above us, I have a straight view right to the sky. My mouth drops. "Oh my God, can you believe that?" Despite the dawn light that streams through, there's also a dark haze over us — a dust that permeates every inch of air space. When I look up it makes me cough.

"Cover your mouth!" Cooper says. I pull my T-shirt over my mouth and start to step up toward the light. I can't resist having a look.

"Zach, no, don't do it!" Cooper yells. "We don't know if anything is structurally safe."

He's got a good point. The last thing we need is everyone surviving the storm only to get hurt trying to get out of here. I turn back toward Coop and we slowly descend the stairwell to check on everyone.

"Please, everyone, check yourself for any possible injuries," Rory is saying. "With all of the debris flying around you might not have even noticed something happen to you." I look everyone over quickly as I go down the stairs. Cooper helps check everyone with me, shining the light wherever it's needed. By some miracle, everyone looks unscathed — the only evidence of the storm on their bodies is the blank, stunned expressions they wear.

"One, two, three ..." I count the people as we walk. Liam and Henry are huddled in tight with Nancy. They look up at me with wide eyes. I give them a reassuring smile.

"It's going to be okay. It's over," I say.

Olivia and Brandon wave us by to let us know they're okay. We get to Peter and Mildred. Peter holds Mildred close to his chest. She looks up at him and asks, "You got Farrah out, right? She's safe?"

Peter sighs and rubs her back. "Farrah is safe, my love."

Mildred visibly relaxes. The lump in my throat forms again. I try to swallow it down over and over again. "You guys aren't hurt?" My voice comes out ragged.

"No, we're just fine," Peter says. "Not sure how George is doing, though."

I nod. "Yeah, I'm anxious to see how he's doing."

I move down to the man in the business suit. He's still wearing handcuffs.

"Are you all right, sir?" I ask.

"Do I look all right?" He's gruff and sour.

I mean, physically he looks fine, but I'm sure being in handcuffs isn't the most fun. I resist giving him a smart aleck comment, even though it's tempting. It's better to just keep on walking.

Rory rubs his head. He looks exhausted. "I'm fine, too, Zach."

I wave thanks and continue down the stairwell. Everyone seems to be fine, which is a huge relief.

Valerie has Ira curled into her chest. He's sucking vigorously on his soother. He flashes me a big smile from behind it and I light up.

"Hi, Ira!" I coo. To my surprise, he even reaches for me, and Valerie passes him over. She looks remarkably calm given the disaster we've just lived through.

"Thank goodness you guys are okay," I say, my voice cracking with emotion. I've grown attached to these people. Ira rests his head on my shoulder and grips my T-shirt collar with his pudgy, dimpled fingers. It makes me melt.

"I think the worst is over," Valerie says. Her relief is palpable. "I don't know what I would have done if something had happened." Her voice catches in her throat.

Ira pulls on my collar and drums his hands playfully against me. I smile and rub his back. His flannel sleeper feels soft and warm against my skin.

"You're a brave little guy," I tell him. "Good job keeping your mom safe."

Valerie smiles.

"With the storm passing, hopefully we'll be able to get out of here soon."

"I hope."

Ira lets go of my shirt and explores my face with his hands. He looks up at me intently, pressing my cheeks.

"I got your fingers!" I say, snapping my jaw at him, pretending I'm going to chomp his fingers. He erupts into a huge belly laugh and the soother hangs loosely from his mouth. We play this game over and over again, and each time he dissolves in a fit of giggles.

"I think that's the best sound in the world," I say. Everyone around us nods in agreement. Ira's joy infuses us all with a little bit of hope.

Ira stops and stares at my gauzed arm.

"Yeah, Zach got an owie," I say.

Ira doesn't try to touch it. He just looks up at me with his big brown eyes.

"Well, buddy, I have to go check on George." I reluctantly hand him back to Valerie. Ira fusses a bit at being passed back, but I wave at him and he tries to wave back.

"That's the first time he's ever waved!!" Valerie's excitement adds to the boost of morale in the room. "He waved to you, Zach!"

"Right on! Next up is the fist bump," I tell him. I wave again and then continue down the stairs behind Cooper. The dust is slowly settling, and starting to allow the morning light from above to penetrate a little. We could almost get by without the flashlight now.

"So glad you boys are okay," Erwin says to Cooper and me.

"How is George?"

George's face is ashen. He looks terrible. He's propped up on a stair and slumped against the wall, and he appears to be sleeping. Or at least I pray he's only sleeping. Erwin sees my dumbstruck look.

"He's just resting. His pulse is weak and thready, but he's still with us."

I lean toward George's face. "George, help is on its way. Just hold on, okay?"

Cooper wrings his hands. His eyes are as bug-eyed as mine as he studies George.

"I've checked outside the door," Erwin tells us. "You're not going to believe your eyes."

And then it occurs to me. Where's Samara?

"Samara? Where is she?"

Erwin looks alarmed. "I haven't seen her. Last time I saw her was quite a while ago. She ran past me up the stairs when you came in together.… Wasn't she up there with you?"

"No!" Terror gnaws at me at once as I realize she must have gone out the upstairs door ahead of me. "That means … she could be out there!" I point to the rest of the mall above the stairwell.

Cooper pulls open the lower door and more light pours in from the gigantic hole in the second-floor ceiling.

"Zach …" Cooper stands stunned. "Come here."

I'm scared to see what awaits me. I step beside Coop and my mouth drops open. Broken slabs of concrete are in piles everywhere — snapped off as effortlessly as bread crumbs. Glass litters the floor in a dazzling array of sparkle. Merchandise from various stores adds colour to the chaos but it's difficult to tell what's what. The security doors have all been blasted off of the storefronts for as far as we can see. They lay like heaps of broken accordions in weird angles. We're standing in a roofless building, and despite the haze that permeates the main floor, too, we can see that the storm is over. The sky is resting.

TIP 014

Neither of us says a word as we take it all in. Cooper puts his arm around me.

"Hey, look, I didn't get to mention how boss it was that you saved George's life."

"Thanks. I wasn't the only one."

"Are you kidding me? You were giving him CPR! Straight up — no joke."

I picture George lying lifeless in that stairwell and myself pumping on his chest hoping for a breath, a movement, anything that would indicate that he was going to be okay — there are no words for a moment like that. A human life hanging in the balance, knowing that you can only do so much ... it's as though time stood still.

"Looks like Bronze Cross really paid off. Not everyone can say they've done something like that." Cooper's words are like a salve to me.

"Yeah. I've never been so scared in my life. But the feeling afterward … I can't even describe it."

"Maybe medicine might be for you after all." Cooper smiles. He of all people has known how unsure I've been of myself.

"Maybe." I play it down but I think this experience has just cemented my career path … *if* I can deliver. I know it's going to be a long and hard road.

"I'm really proud of you," Cooper tells me. "And jealous. I don't think I could do something like that."

"That's the thing! I think Samara was right. No one really knows what they're capable of until they're in a desperate situation."

"I think we've had our fair share of crazy for a while," Cooper says, laughing. "I'm thinking a hard-core *Fortnite* session is in order once we get out of here."

"Definitely!" I say. "And some Doritos. I hope my mom lets me chill for like a week at least after this."

"Yeah, I'd say you earned that."

"Remember when we tried to convince my parents that gaming was really just preparing us for our futures?"

Cooper laughs. "Yup." We were about twelve at the time and my mom was concerned that I was spending too much time on electronics — as though I were different from any other kid my age on the planet. So we came up with a plan to change their minds about gaming.

Coop and I researched the benefits of playing video games; we dressed up in suits and ties and pleaded our case. We must've impressed her with our stats: how gaming can help ease pain, how it may slow the aging process, how it reduces stress, how the vivid displays and immersive experience can lead to an interest in history.

"Remember how she said she thought I was becoming a recluse? I showed her that I had no trouble making social connections because I had you and twenty-eight friends on Discord."

"Twenty-eight. That's awesome." Cooper laughs. "My favourite was when you told her that you'd need to improve your hand-eye coordination if you were going to become a doctor."

"Yeah, that was the clincher!" I chuckle.

With all of the negative media surrounding screen time, we thought it was important to point out the good things it had done for us. Besides the benefits we'd researched, gaming had other positive effects on our lives. It had become an outlet for us to reinvent ourselves and gain confidence in a new world that didn't have the same social parameters as the one we were actually living in. In the real world we were always feeling like we didn't quite fit in, but online under our gamertags, we could be anything we wanted to be. The playing field felt more even.

It had also become a creative outlet and a stress reliever for me. Some kids draw, others play sports or go into drama; gaming was my way of putting my stamp on the world, even if it was virtual. And after seeing me code, even my mom couldn't argue with that.

We even convinced my mom to try *Fortnite* and she had to admit that she liked playing it a lot more than she had expected to. I learned two rules when it came to playing with her: never ever troll her and always let her get the upper hand.

"When she started playing she finally understood why we couldn't just shut it off randomly wherever we were in the game."

"Yeah, that was pretty cool," I say.

"Your mom is so awesome," Cooper says. I nod. A lump develops in my throat. We both grow quiet again. It's hard not to imagine the worst. Our city looks like a wasteland from up here.

"They are all going to be fine, Zach." Cooper must be thinking the same things I am.

"I know." My voice is ragged. It's just that some of our group aren't fine, like George, for example, and we have no idea what's been taking place *outside* of this building. What if they aren't okay?

And then I remember: "Samara!" Thinking about her still out there makes me want to throw up.

"What do you mean?" Cooper asks.

"I thought she was in the stairwell the whole time but she's not here. She must've gone out the upstairs door just before I came out to find you."

"You mean she was out there during the storm?" Cooper's eyes grow wide with alarm. It doesn't look like anything could have survived the storm out here. "Samara!!" he yells.

We hear nothing.

I join in. "Samara!!" I can't handle the idea that something might have happened to her.

"There's no way …" Cooper says carefully, trying to convince himself. "She wouldn't have stayed out there."

"Yeah, but look how fast the tornado hit. Maybe she tried to get back here in time but never made it." We're both stunned at the thought.

The debris is piled high, and the mess of tangled metal and concrete and wood is blocking any sort of path. There's a total absence of sound, as though the world has been put on mute.

"This is eerie," Cooper says. If the dark mall looked haunting before the storm, it's a hundred times creepier now. Although light is trying to filter in, the destruction is horror at its best.

"We no longer have outside contact," Erwin tells us. He holds up his radio. "I've got nothing."

"But they know we're here, right? It's just a matter of time," Cooper says.

"I don't think we're getting out anytime soon." I point to the mess outside the door. "It's going to take them a while to get through that in order to get to us."

"I don't think we can wait," Erwin says. "George is pretty unstable. I'd prefer to get him over to the food court doors somehow. That's where I told the paramedics to enter the building."

"So, what are you saying? We should carry George over there?" I ask. That seems like a pretty tall order given the state of the rubble inside the mall.

"How do we even know that the building is structurally sound?" Cooper asks.

"Well, we don't," Erwin says.

Cooper gulps. "I don't think this is such a hot idea."

"And what about everyone else?" I ask. "Are they supposed to stay here or follow?"

Erwin chews his lip. "I think we all stand a better chance if we can get to those food court doors. Maybe we can find something to make some kind of stretcher."

I raise my eyebrows. I have no MacGyver abilities that would help me make a human-worthy carrying vessel of any sort. But Coop, on the other hand, has been a Boy Scout for years. "You could do that, Coop." I pat him on the back.

"Uh, I don't know about that," Cooper says, incredulous.

"George's condition is worsening. If he's going to stand a chance, we have to get him out of here now." Erwin's voice is grave.

"We'll go check things out," I say. "C'mon, Coop."

Cooper reluctantly follows me out of the stairwell and into the main mall area. The whole building shifts in minute ways — a shudder, a groan, a scratch of metal against metal. It's a symphony of building materials settling into one another.

I don't know where to step or where to look first. Twisted rebar juts out of concrete slabs like spikes. The small areas of floor space that remain free from debris are at least six inches deep with murky water. The water is ice-cold and it makes the floor slippery.

"There's hail in here, too." Cooper points to random golf ball–sized pieces of ice sprinkled among the mess.

I survey the scene. It reminds me of the Scorch in the Maze Runner series: an abandoned city in ruins, where numerous obstacles and potential dangers await. And, somehow, we're harvesting materials out of this wreckage.

"We need rope. And something hard to lay George on."

"All I see is metal, glass, and concrete." I can't fathom how we're going to be able to put something together.

"What's that over there?" Cooper points to a big round-ed piece of something solid-looking and aqua blue sticking up out from the wreckage. I can't tell until I see the store-front about ten feet away. It's Surfer City, the chain store ironically located in the middle of the land-locked prai-ries where no surf waves can be found for at least 1,200 kilometres.

"A surfboard?" I guess.

"We have a place that sells surfboards?" Cooper asks, smirking.

"Maybe it's a paddleboard."

"That would make more sense." Saskatchewan has roughly 100,000 lakes, and paddleboards are a favourite out on the water.

I test the stability of the pile of concrete in front of me and decide that it feels pretty good. I start to pick my way along the jagged landscape. Cooper follows me.

"Careful, there's glass everywhere!"

As we get closer, we see that the entire store looks as though it's been put through a blender. I try to pry the paddleboard out from under the debris, but it won't come loose.

"Here, let me get in there, too," Cooper says. He scoots in beside me and together we pull as hard as we can on the moulded fibreglass. It wiggles free and the force of our pulling sends us both flat onto our backs on the jagged concrete.

"Ouch!" Cooper yells. I watch as he pulls a three-inch piece of glass from his left hip. I wince both at the glass and my own pain. My back has taken a beating during this ordeal: getting knocked into the stairs, sitting for so long, and crouching down during the storm.

"Will this work?" I ask him, breathless.

"Yes. But we need something to secure him to the board with. It's way too risky just laying him on there if we're going to try to walk through this mess."

I look around but see nothing that would help us. I try to remember the stores in the mall.

"There's a camping place somewhere," I say. "They'll have rope."

"That's right. The Woodsman."

"Isn't it on the other side?"

Cooper tries to get his bearings. "No. It's beside that makeup store. I think it's just around these elevators actually." But there isn't much less debris in that direction either.

"You boys okay?" Erwin yells out the door.

"Yeah, we're good!" I call back. I watch as Cooper makes his way to the other side of the elevators with the agility of a monkey while I try to make it to solid ground with the grace of a bull in a china shop.

I hold on to the paddleboard firmly and slosh over to the elevators by stepping into the open crevasses I see. My feet are growing numb from the shock of the sludgy, cold water.

A few minutes later, Coop returns with a package of rope and a sleeping bag. He uses the sleeping bag to give his hands support as he manoeuvres through the maze of debris.

"The security gate was blown right off of that store, too," he tells me. "If we're stuck here any longer, there's a whole bunch of stuff we can use to help us." He jumps toward me and lands in the water with a satisfying splash. "Let's start Operation: Rescue George."

"Good job, boys!" Erwin says when he sees us.

"So, we strap him onto here," says Cooper. "The sleeping bag will help keep him warm and protected. But it's going to be really tricky getting him out of here."

"We've got to give it a try," I say.

"Is this such a good idea?" Valerie steps in. "What about the rest of us?"

"I think we should all go. Safety in numbers, remember?" Erwin says.

"But we know we're safe in here," she says.

"George is deteriorating. His best chance is to get out of here and into the hands of the people who can help him as soon as we can get him there." George's skin has taken on an even greyer pallor.

"I understand, but aren't we taking a big risk walking through an obliterated building?"

Erwin nods.

We all ponder that thought.

"We gotta save George," I say. "He kept us safe. We owe the same to him."

No one argues, but there is an uneasiness among us.

Erwin makes the final decision.

"Okay, then. Let's get him loaded."

TIP #15

Even if the princess doesn't need to be
rescued, she still likes a knight

Even though we're busy with George, I can't stop thinking of Samara. I wonder if she's trapped somewhere, hurt.
Cooper must be wondering the same thing.

"It's okay, Zach. We'll find her."

"Yeah," I say. A lump forms in my throat. George
doesn't stir when we load him onto the paddleboard.
Although he's breathing, he remains unconscious. Erwin
covers him with the sleeping bag and then Cooper ties the
rope around him and the board multiple times.

"What's that saying? If you can't tie knots, tie lots?"
I tease, but Cooper is experienced in knot-tying. I once
attended a scout camp with him during "bring-a-friend"
week and the group activity had been to make a rope
bridge that the entire group could walk on safely. Cooper
knows what he's doing.

"He *is* still breathing, right?" Cooper asks. Erwin nods
but he's clearly concerned. Cooper addresses the group.

"Okay, everyone, I want you to move slowly and carefully. There's a lot of glass and twisted metal outside. It's very easy to slip. Help each other out whenever you can."

Just then, Joaquin and A.J. appear. "Let us go ahead," Joaquin says. "We'll try to clear a path."

Although there's significant danger in trying to move the debris, it's George's best chance. It's also the safest way for Mildred and Peter and Valerie and Ira to get out of here.

"It's going to be hard to see metal and glass through that gross water," Cooper says. He's right. It's like a grey soup, and it has a funky, dank smell.

I turn to see Valerie closing her eyes and mumbling to herself. It takes me a moment to realize that she's praying. When she finishes she makes a quick sign of the cross and then kisses the top of Ira's head. I give her a supportive smile but she doesn't smile back. Worry is etched into her face.

Rory makes his way to the bottom of the stairs to talk to Erwin before they set out.

"What about me?" I hear a familiar bitter voice. It's the man in the business suit. Our resident thief. "Are you ready to take these things off yet?"

Rory gives us a mischievous grin. "Not a chance," he whispers, and then turns to the man. "You're the least of my worries at the moment."

The man swears under his breath and starts banging the cuffs loudly and repeatedly against the handrail, obviously hoping to annoy everyone. We all try our best to ignore him.

"You guys are doing a great job," I tell Rory. "It's not easy taking care of a bunch of cranky strangers."

"When I signed up to become a security guard I didn't realize how hard it'd be," Rory says. "People think we're just basically rent-a-cops, but we deal with a lot more than you'd think."

After everything we've been through, I don't doubt it.

Peter comes down the stairs toward me. He looks troubled. "Zach, Mildred's not going to be able to make it out of here on her own."

I nod.

"We're going to need someone to carry her," he continues. "And I'm afraid I can't do it any longer."

"I know," I say, trying to reassure him. "How about when we get George to the doors, we come back for Mildred with the paddleboard and transport her the same way?"

Peter considers this. "I think that might be best." His face registers relief. "I'll go and talk to her and try to prepare her."

"We've got a path started!" A.J. yells back to us. I glance out the doorway and sure enough, there's a path about twenty feet long and at least a foot wide that we can shuffle through with the paddleboard.

"Yes!" I say excitedly. This feels like a major win considering the night we've just had.

"Can you take a side?" Erwin asks me. Cooper has taken the front of the paddleboard and Erwin's on the right-hand side. I make eye contact with Valerie, knowing I'm going to be leaving her and Ira alone for a while. She nods at me and waves me on. I grip the side across from Erwin, but we soon realize that there's only room for two people to carry George. The pathway only allows for someone at the front and someone at the back.

"Can you take this, Zach?" Erwin asks. I nod. Cooper and I make a much more even match. Erwin is an older gentleman himself, and his short, rounded stature makes carrying George a challenge for him.

Together Cooper and I shuffle slowly down the pathway. Carrying George is a lot harder than I expected. My arms shake from the weight. Water sloshes around us and the odd piece of wreckage keeps sliding into our path, causing one of us to trip. It's a bumpy ride for George, and slow-going. In minutes my hands start to cramp, and they keep sliding from the paddleboard because they're coated with sweat. My breath becomes laboured. Cooper has it even rougher than me because he's facing forward, gripping the paddleboard behind his back.

I marvel at Cooper's iron grip and his ability to guide us. He must be in much better shape than me because I feel like I'm going to drop George and pass out. We get to where A.J. and Joaquin are standing and see that the rest of the corridor is relatively clear from here on in.

"Oh, thank goodness!" I say, signalling to Cooper to take a break. We lower George to the ground as gently as we can. I wipe the sweat from my forehead and peel my shirt away from my chest; it's sticky and wet.

"Want us to take over?" A.J. asks, and Cooper and I nod gratefully. To my surprise, Cooper looks as bagged as I am.

I look back to see Liam and Henry, Nancy, Olivia, Brandon, the two sales women from Designer Dresses, and most of the others making their way through the water toward us. I yearn to see Samara walking with the rest of the group, but it feels like a pipe dream. I have to find her; I have to know that she's okay.

"I have to look for Samara!" I say to Cooper.

He nods but he looks exhausted. "Where should we start?"

"I don't know. Anywhere at this point." The destruction is overwhelming. I try not to picture her pinned under the debris but it's hard to imagine where else she'd be. How did I not notice that she wasn't with us? All along I thought she was safe in the stairs. Now I find out that she was on the second floor and that I was the closest to her of everyone in the group the whole time.

"I'm going back," I decide. "I'm going to check upstairs."

"Zach, the door was blown right off. There's no way she was upstairs."

"That's the thing — I think she was!"

"Oh God," Cooper mutters. He's imagining the same horrors I am.

I make my way past the other members of our group, jumping through the water in the pathway, and get to the stairwell door in record time. Suddenly I'm a lot more agile than I thought I was. I bound up the stairs, past Ira's stroller, the handcuffed man, Rory, Peter, and Mildred.

"Are you all right?" Peter asks me, concerned.

"It's Samara," I say breathlessly. "She's missing."

I race to the top where the steel door used to be. A gentle breeze makes some of the lighter debris flap in the wind. I'm standing on the second floor of the biggest mall in the city, and because the roof and part of the wall has been blown off, I can see everything outside. From here I get an open-air, panoramic view of part of my city — the city where I was born and raised. I don't even recognize it.

Trees have been snapped into jagged blades. A new neighbourhood being built just west of the mall has been wiped clean — the only evidence it ever existed is the exposed foundations left in the houses' places. At once everything is familiar and unfamiliar — a battle in my mind between what once was and what I see before me. The two images are so incongruent that I blink to make sure I'm not hallucinating. Balls of coloured metal litter the landscape around the mall. It takes me a moment to decipher that they're cars and trucks, steel vehicles crushed as easily as aluminum cans.

The dense line of trees that borders the new development has been reduced to barren splinters. Even parts of the road have risen in great heaves toward the sky. I can see the bridge from here. It's been washed clean away, and the water runs fiercely past where it used to be. The landscape is entirely different in the storm's wake. It's as though nothing in the storm's path was sacred.

I turn my attention back to the interior of the mall. Most of the second floor has been ripped up and carried away by the storm. There are gaping holes in the floor. I'm unsure about stepping out any farther, knowing that so much of the floor has collapsed onto the main floor below.

"Samara?" I call out. My voice feels lost in the cavernous air space around me. "Samara, are you there?"

I hear nothing. The pit in the bottom of my stomach turns into a boulder. I want to vomit.

"Samara, can you hear me?"

I pause to listen for a response but get nothing.

I step out a bit, praying that I don't fall through. It feels solid and sure, so I continue, stepping around the elevator and stairwell entrances to the other side.

"Samara?"

This time I hear something. I scan the debris and the blown-out storefronts. Looking for a human in this mess is a bit like playing a sick game of *Where's Waldo?* and it's a game I'm not up for.

"Can you call out again? I'm trying to find you!" I say, unsure of who or what I may find but hoping it's Samara.

"Help!" I hear.

I think of all of the strategy games I've played — how your character must explore dark landscapes and difficult terrain all the time. I just never thought I'd be doing something like this in real life. This mall is a veritable wasteland.

I continue to examine all of the wreckage. Then I see a bright flash of colour. It's her orange T-shirt ... and a purple boot. It's her. It's Samara.

Without thinking I run toward her, no longer assessing the danger around me. I'm on a mission to get her no matter what the circumstance. She's gripping a post between two storefronts. The heavy glass pane from a store's security door lies in a twisted pile over one of Samara's legs … and something else.

It's Betty, Samara's mom. The glass covers her from the chest down.

"Zach!" Samara is breathing hard and tears run down her face. Her face is dusted with grey streaks of dirt. The stray wisps of her hair jut out in every direction. Even her clothing is torn in places. I think she's both laughing and crying from the relief of seeing me.

"Are you hurt?" My heart is racing.

"No. I don't think so."

Her mom watches the two of us.

"What about your mom?" I ask. I don't know what to call her. I don't even know Samara's last name.

"I'm okay," she says quietly.

"We're both pinned underneath this thing," Samara says, trying to push the security gate off. It creaks and slides just inches off of her. "I can't get it myself."

"Let me help," I say, positioning myself so that I can get a better grip on it. "On three."

We count together. "One … two … three!" I bend my knees and get myself under it so that I can lift it straight up. Shards of glass rain down on Samara's legs. Dots of blood appear where the pieces of glass have nicked her. When I get the gate high enough, I toss it away from us.

"Forget the storm. *You* are the Incredible Hulk." Samara is beaming.

"I thought you said he was a crazed behemoth."

"And I thought you said he was a genius," she reminds me.

"I'll take that," I say, pulling her to her feet. We both reach for her mom's arms and help her up.

"Thank you," Betty says. She teeters as she tries to stand but smiles at me gratefully.

"Mom, this is Zach. Zach, this is my mom, Betty."

"Pleased to meet you," I say, holding out my hand. Betty shakes it and then puts her arm around Samara. She looks relieved to be with her daughter.

"And Alec?" I ask. "Where is he?"

Samara's face sours. She glances at Betty, and says, "We're not sure and we don't care. We're making a new start." She and Betty share a meaningful look that I can't quite decipher. I hope Samara's right. There's nothing I want more for her than to have a good mom — the kind of mom that might go to work every day, make a turkey dinner, bake cookies, read stories, and be a role model for her child, but most importantly, love her. A mom like mine.

"How are your legs?" I ask. Both of her legs have been cut up.

"Just a few scratches," Samara says dismissively.

"We have stuff to get you cleaned up," I remind her. "The first aid supplies are still in the stairwell. We're all moving down to the food court. We're hoping that George will get access to help sooner from there. A.J. and Joaquin cleared a path for us and Cooper and I carried George on a paddleboard. We're going to take Mildred that way, too."

I guide the ladies back toward the stairwell so that we can join the others. Samara and her mom stop abruptly when they see the wall that's been blown out leaving a gaping hole and the view of the city. They take in the scene.

"Oh my," Betty says.

"It looks like the apocalypse out there," Samara says. She's right. It does. They survey the same things I did: the washed-out bridge, the decimated trees, the homes that have been swept clean off of their foundations.

I wait as they absorb what's happened around them.

"The tornado did all of this," Betty says to no one in particular. It's hard to believe that seven minutes of a swirling vortex could be capable of this level of destruction.

"My bag!" Samara says. "It's still back there!" She points to where I found her and her mom.

"It's okay, I'll get it," I say. I step back through the debris to where they were trapped. Sure enough, Samara's bag is there. Her sketchbook peeks out from the top of the bag. I reach down to scoop it up, and I see Samara's mom's backpack nearby. Something orange catches my eye on the ground a few feet away. I use my foot to clear some of the metal so that I can get a better look. I uncover several prescription bottles — some open and empty. Various pills also dot the floor in places.

Does this mean it was Alec and Betty who looted the pharmacy in Shoppers Drug Mart? Betty must've realized she didn't have her bag either when Samara mentioned missing hers, but she didn't ask me to retrieve it. Did she leave it behind intentionally? I picture how happy Samara looked when her mom put her arm around her. How they talked about a new start. I pull the metal back to cover the area. Some things are better left behind.

I pass Samara's bag to her. On the way down the stairs, we pass Peter, Mildred, Rory, and the man in the business suit. Thankfully, he's given up clanging his cuffs against the handrail, but he doesn't look any happier.

"We'll get you with the others," I tell Betty and Samara. I show them the path that A.J. and Joaquin carved for us and they follow me to where the floor is clear from debris.

"Just follow this. See where Gamer's Haven is? Turn left at the end there to get to the food court. I'll be there soon."

Samara takes her mom's hand and together they wade through the water toward the food court. Seeing Gamer's Haven ahead of me makes me choke up thinking of Chris. Whatever happened overnight, I hope he's safe with his wife and his new baby. I guess time will tell.

I decide to go back to wait with Peter and Mildred. She's probably really scared about getting carried out of here, and maybe I can help distract her or keep her calm. I teeter carefully down the path, careful to avoid any of the juts of metal and concrete that seem to have tumbled closer to each other, narrowing our trail.

I'm incredibly relieved to have found Samara, and even more to know that she has her mom right now — in the way that she needs her. I know it's not this easy, that it'll take time and may not last, but it's a step in the right direction. I hear sirens in the distance. I smile. Medical care is coming. George will get what he needs. Hopefully my parents are somewhere nearby, safe and waiting for me. The thought that I may see them soon thrills me.

"Zach!" It's Valerie.

"Why are you coming back this way? Are you okay?"

"We're fine!" Valerie assures me. She's balancing Ira on her hip. "Actually, we're more than fine! My husband, Joshua, is here — Ira's dad. Turns out he was waiting out the storm at the bank down the street. He was nearby the whole time."

"Oh, that's so awesome!" I tell her. "You get to go home?"

"I hope so. If we find a way there," Valerie says. "I just had to come back and say thanks. And I guess goodbye."

"Here, I'll walk back with you. Make sure you get there safely."

"You're such a great young man, Zach," she says seriously.

"Thanks," I say shyly.

Ira reaches out to me again. Valerie hands him over to me. "He just loves you!" she says, laughing. I pretend to chomp on his fingers and he dissolves into giggles once more. The sound is contagious, and it's just the kind of sound we all need to hear right now.

Samara sees us coming and runs up to join us. She watches as Ira sneaks his little hands near my mouth only to see me pretend to eat them up.

"Can I come see him sometime?" I ask Valerie. Ira's such a cool little kid.

"Of course!" Valerie says. "He'd love that. I'd love that!" Valerie digs in her bag for a pen and something to write on. She scribbles down her phone number on a paper scrap and hands it to me.

"Awesome. And if you ever need a babysitter …" I say. "I know I have a lot to learn still but —"

"I'll help him," Samara offers.

Valerie gives me a knowing smile. "I think you'll be just great with him," she assures me.

"Take care, little buddy!" I say, handing him back to his mom. I wave at him again and he tries his best to flap his hand back at me. They scurry off to find Valerie's husband.

"That kid adores you," Samara says.

I grin. "He's a pretty cool kid."

"He's not the only one who —" Samara is cut off by the sound of sirens approaching. We race toward the food court table where they've placed the paddleboard to keep George off the water that blankets the ground. He's still unconscious, but he's breathing.

Two paramedics step through the food court doors with their kits. I take a moment to survey the scene. While some of the storefronts and tables have been blown clear, others remain perfectly in place, unaffected by the storm. "Weird," Samara says.

Erwin calls for me so that we can explain the timeline and what we did to get George breathing again. The paramedic takes George's vitals and continues to ask us questions.

He's calm and professional — and I realize that I'm in awe of his composure. I hope I can gain the skills to tackle medical emergencies the same way one day. I've gotten a taste of what it's like to help save people and I want more. I want to learn and grow and become as adept at it as this paramedic seems to be.

"And you are?" the paramedic asks me. His eyes are kind, and his smile is reassuring.

"Zach."

"How old are you, Zach?" he asks.

"Fifteen."

He whistles and nods his head in surprise. "You did an incredible thing today, Zach." He pats me on the back. His name tag says his name is Matt.

"Thanks, but it was a group effort," I say.

"How do you know CPR?" he asks.

"Training to be a lifeguard. But your job looks pretty cool, too," I say.

He laughs lightly. "Yeah, it can be pretty cool. Sounds like you're well on your way."

I step out of the way as the two paramedics talk and then load George onto a proper stretcher. "Haven't seen that before," Matt says, smiling and pointing to the paddleboard.

"Anyone else hurt?" the other paramedic asks. He points at my arm. "I think we should have a look at that."

"It's fine," I say. "Just a little scratch. The gauze is overkill." It still hurts but I don't want to be the focus here. "She's going to need some assistance," I say, pointing to Samara. Blood has run down her legs in thin streams from her cuts. He motions for her to have a seat on one of the food court chairs and examines her more closely.

"We've also got an elderly couple still in the stairwell," I tell them. "I think they might need some attention."

Just then, two police officers enter through the smashed-in doors.

"Is everyone here accounted for?" a male officer asks. Everyone looks around trying to gauge who might be missing.

"No," Erwin says grimly. He takes the officer to the side to fill him in about those still missing — Chris, and even Alec — and about the resident jewellery thief among us, the handcuffed business man waiting in the stairwell with Rory.

"Not only that, but I've got two stores that I know of that have been broken into by looters. I don't know who's responsible for them, but there could be even more. We weren't as secure as we would've liked," Erwin says, indicating the food court doors. "Plus, we were in the stairwell for the majority of the storm. It was safer that way."

The officer nods. "In a crisis most of us look for safety, but unfortunately some people see disasters as opportunity."

The idea that the looters could have been roaming the mall the whole time we were stuck makes the hair on the back of my neck stand up. I hope the police are able to catch whoever was doing the break-ins.

"Is he going to be okay?" I ask the paramedics as I bid George goodbye.

"You guys have done a great job keeping him stable," the second paramedic says. I know they probably aren't sure themselves of George's prognosis at this point, but I'm relieved that George is in good hands.

"How will you get to the hospital with the bridge out?" I ask.

"Oh, he's going by helicopter," Matt tells me.

"That wasn't an ambulance we heard?" Cooper asks.

"That was the police. With that bridge out, our only access point is the grid road — and it's been jammed with cars. Now that the tornado is over with, we'll have him at the hospital in about ten minutes," Matt assures us.

"That was some kind of tornado," I say.

"They're calling it an EF5," Matt says. "Only the second in Canada's history, but they're calling this one the worst. By the looks of this building, I'd say you were all very lucky." The paramedics bid us goodbye, and they roll the stretcher out of the mall.

I remember from school how tornadoes are rated on a damage scale, named after a Dr. Fujita who studied them. It rates the severity of a tornado based on wind speeds and the amount of destruction it leaves behind. The magnitude could be ranked as F0 to F5, with F5 being the worst. Dr. Fujita's scale later became the EF-Scale, or the Enhanced Fujita Scale. If Matt's report is correct, and we've just experienced a real EF5 tornado, then we had just lived through one of Mother Nature's biggest threats to human survival.

"Saskatoon has declared a state of emergency," I hear the officer tell the group. "The Red Cross is sending rescue teams to come and help. There are tent hospitals being set up in parking lots all over the city to treat the injured.

We'll have to get some engineers in here to help remove the wreckage — it looks like the roof got blown clear off this place."

"Pretty much," Erwin says.

"I don't know how you're going to find anyone in there," I say. "It's full of concrete and metal and glass."

"We have our ways," the officer says. "We've got special cameras and life detectors that we can use. We'll even be sending our dogs through here."

The rest of us listen intently, impressed.

"We should go and get Mildred now," Erwin says, holding up the paddleboard.

"Only the people who can help carry," the officer says. "Everyone else is to remain here."

I look for Samara and our eyes meet. This time Cooper is across from me and his back is to her, so I know that her gaze is meant for me. It feels electric, a laser beam gaining magnetic energy as the two of us stare at each other. She waves at me. My hands turn cold and clammy, my stomach somersaults.

"Zach, let's go!" Cooper calls out.

He's already heading back into the mess with A.J., Joaquin, Erwin, and the police officer to help get Mildred. I wave and jog toward the group. Water splays wildly as I slosh through it, drawing attention to myself. I turn to glance at Samara one more time and this time she's laughing. For just having been in the most terrifying situation of my life, this particular moment on the same day feels pretty amazing.

TIP #16

Accept setbacks as another
part of the journey

The officer leads the way through the water. A.J., Joaquin, Erwin, Cooper, and I all follow. We'll need to take turns carrying Mildred, and Peter might need assistance, too. The officer will be busy with Rory and our jewellery thief.

When we get to the centre of the mall where the debris is piled, the officer stops and stares in disbelief. "I can't even believe my eyes right now," he says. "You are all lucky to be alive."

We nod, remembering the terrifying storm, the deafening roar of the tornado, the uncertainty about whether or not we'd be swept away in the black vortex. I follow close behind the others, eager to see how Peter and Mildred are doing. It takes us a while to step through the pathway.

"Are we going to be able to navigate this with the paddleboard?" A.J. asks. The path is shrinking by the minute as the debris slips back toward the open space he and Joaquin cleared.

"I'm not sure it's safe for you guys to follow," the officer says. "We don't need anyone else getting hurt. Nothing here looks stable." The sounds of metal and glass creaking and settling makes for an eerie symphony.

"You aren't going to be able to do this alone," Erwin says. "We need to get them out of here as soon as we can and who knows when more help will arrive."

The officer hesitates.

"It's not going to be easy," Erwin agrees. "Let's just try to get this done as quickly as we can."

The officer opens the steel stairwell door and I hear a collective sigh of relief from those left in the stairwell, except maybe the business man, although I can't see his face.

As I step into the small open floor area in front of the stairwell, a large piece of debris falls from the ceiling onto my head. I yelp from the pain when it connects, knocking me to my hands and knees. The object makes a loud clatter as it bounces off of the tile floor.

Everyone turns.

"Zach?" Cooper says, concerned. "What was that?"

"I don't know," I say from the floor. "Something just fell from the ceiling."

"Are you okay?" he asks. Everyone gathers around me.

"Yeah, I'm fine." There's a sharp piercing pain on the side of my head.

"What was it?" he asks.

"I don't know? A rock? A piece of metal?"

We all look around for whatever hit me, but there's so much stuff strewn around already, it's hard to tell if there's been a new item added to the mix.

"I bet it was this." Cooper lifts a thick chunk of metal from just beyond the crown of my head.

"It's nothing. Just a bump on the head," I say. I try to get myself up but it's harder than I expect. My back sears with pain as well. I slump down onto my butt.

"Take it easy," Cooper says. "Don't rush."

I try to stand again but my body feels weak and unsteady. My head spins and I reel back.

"Zach, maybe you should stay down." Cooper places his hand on my good arm.

"I'm fine. Let's go." I brush Cooper's hand away and rise to my feet again. The room spins and white spots blur my vision. I stumble backward.

"Okay, that's it. You're staying put," Cooper orders. He shoves me down to sitting.

"I just need a minute," I say, but then I'm not really sure.

"Don't move," Edwin says.

I don't know how I feel so disoriented. "Are you dizzy?" I ask.

Cooper shakes his head. "No, I'm fine. But you're clearly not."

"Let's lie him down," Edwin instructs.

The room tilts again and this time my stomach roils. A cold sweat blankets me. I put my head in my hands to try to minimize the spinning sensation. Once I've steadied myself I realize that my right hand feels warm and sticky. I pull it away and see that it's wet with bright red blood.

Cooper gasps.

I touch the area again and come away with fresh blood.

"Oh my God!" Cooper's mouth hangs open.

I stare back at him, dazed. I blink a few times as I take in his face.

"Zach is hurt! Really badly!" Cooper screams.

"I'm fine …" I stammer, but even I'm not so sure anymore. Things become blurry again. Bile somersaults in my stomach. I fight the urge to vomit.

"You need to stay still," Cooper says sharply. He takes off his hoodie and presses it into a ball so that I can use it as a pillow. "Lie back on this," he instructs. I try to settle backward but everything spins and I clutch my head again. Cooper guides me down and sets me gently onto his hoodie.

"I'm trying to get a better look," Cooper says. I can feel his cool fingers gently combing through the hair on the right side of my head. He's studying the top of my head closely. I shut my eyes for a brief second. The darkness is soothing. My head feels like it's been swirling in a blender — a combination of pain and disequilibrium. I relish being still. I think again of my parents and of Marshall and where they might be right now. I wonder if the tornado has touched down in several places or if by some miracle the mall is the only place hit. My mom's face comes into view. She's leaning over me.

"Zach, I'm so proud of you," she says softly. "You've done amazing things today."

I nod and reach for her neck so that I can hug her.

"It's okay. Just rest."

"Mom! Mom!" I reach for her again. Instead of holding me tight, she tries to pry my arms from her neck.

"Don't go!" I plead. I just want the safety and comfort of her right now.

"Zach!" I hear. "Zach!" The sound is familiar, but it's not my mom's voice. I try to follow the sound. I work at opening my eyes. I want so desperately to feel my mom's arms around me. I start to see some light again.

"Mom?" I say to the light.

"What should we do?" I see the faint outlines of what look like heads close together.

"There's really nothing we *can* do," I hear. "We'll have to wait for medical care."

The heads nod and grow quiet. It dawns on me that this might be serious. A mistake like this might cost me the game. There is no reset button, no extra lives that let me start back at the original checkpoint. I fall into sleep again.

My mind plays a movie of weird dreams while I rest. A reunion with my parents and brother. The looters chasing me through the dark mall, except I'm tripping on debris and I can't outrun them. The skunk that scared Cooper and me; it's rabid and trying to attack me. Me and Samara alone in the stairwell, arguing.

"I didn't want you to know the truth about my family," Samara says.

"You didn't even give me a chance. But you shared it with Cooper?"

"Don't you see? I really liked you. I didn't want that to change your opinion of me! I was worried that you wouldn't want to be with someone whose family was so messed up."

"I'm into *you*. Your family is pretty secondary to that."

"You don't know my family," Samara says, raising her eyebrows. "It's not that easy."

"I know all I need to know to figure out whether or not I want to be with you," I reply.

"Then in the stairwell … you comfort me and almost kiss me and then run off?!"

"I thought you were into Cooper."

"I didn't pull away!" Samara raises her voice.

"I thought Cooper was into you, too. When he came in, I couldn't do that to him." I may be totally into Samara but I'm not going to sacrifice a ten-year friendship for some girl I just met, no matter how cool she seems.

"But you could do it to me?"

"Cooper's been my best friend forever," I say. "It's different. I had just met you."

"And what about when we were sitting by ourselves on the bench? You made it pretty clear that we were just friends."

"You were the one who pulled away that time. I said it because that's what I thought you wanted."

"Well, you thought wrong." Samara shakes her head. "I feel like every time I got close, you pushed me away."

Tears build in Samara's eyes. It makes me feel awful. She was trying to tell me and I was too wrapped up in myself and her and Cooper's suspected romance that I couldn't see things for what they were.

"So, you're saying you feel the same way about me?"

In my dream Samara turns and runs out of the stairwell. The metal door slams so loudly I jump. I never get the answer.

TIP #17

My eyelids flutter open. At first, I notice the stark white walls of the inside of the stairwell. We're still in the mall. My insides churn with anxiety. How can we still be in the same spot? I blink a few times to try to get my bearings. Maybe I'm mistaken.

I try to move but my legs won't stretch. I flail them outward but they hit something hard.

"Zach, stay still," I hear Cooper say.

"What's going on?" I ask. "Where are we?"

"We're still beside the stairwell."

"Is everyone here?"

"No. Most of them are back in the food court. We're waiting things out."

"Waiting what out? I thought the storm had moved on."

"It did, but it's not that simple."

I want so badly to uncurl my legs, but they meet the wall instead. I flex them out again, clumsily.

"Zach, try to hold still."

"Why?"

"You took a hard hit."

At first, I don't feel anything at all. My hands go to my head and pat my face and hair. My right hand comes up bright with blood again.

"This? It's nothing," I say.

"No, it's something," Cooper says. "You've been doing all sorts of weird things since it happened."

"How long was I out for?"

"I'm not quite sure. An hour? Maybe more?"

"Serious?"

"Yeah. You need to stay still." Cooper presses on my shoulder gently to keep me from rising. I push against him. Then my back and head ache — a steady throb that makes me wince. I shut my eyes again.

"He's awake?" It's Rory. I open my eyes and see that he and Erwin are standing over me.

"Yes. He wants to get up but I told him he has to stay put."

Concern is etched on everybody's face.

"Zach?!" I recognize the soft voice. She leans over me, her mane-like ponytail cascading over her shoulder and dangling onto my face. It tickles my cheek.

"Hi, Samara," I whisper. My voice has gone hoarse on me. I don't know if it's because of my injury or because she's so close to me.

"Glad you're awake," she says. In this moment, the freckles that dot her nose and cheeks are what I notice most when she smiles at me. Then I see her eyes — they're green and sparkling. I do a double-take; it almost looks as though she has tears. Her face is creased with worry. Her concern for me sends a thrill through me that I can't quite explain. It's excitement, anticipation, caring, desire, relief, gratitude — everything I feel about the thought of us being together.

"You're here," I manage.

"I never left," she says softly.

"You've been here the whole time?"

"As soon as I found out you were hurt." I feel her hand close around mine.

"Look, I'm sorry."

"No need to apologize, Zach."

"I didn't tell you how I felt about you."

"I wasn't exactly honest with you either," Samara admits. My eyelids get heavy again and I fight the urge to close them. Samara squeezes my hand and I drift off.

TIP #18

Kiss her like you mean it

The next time I open my eyes, I'm being loaded onto a stretcher. At first the figures around me are blurry, but I blink a few times and things come into focus.

"You're awake!" It's Matt, the paramedic, again.

I manage a weak smile. "I'm trying," I say. Cooper, Samara, Rory, and Erwin all stand nearby. "George?"

"He's stable," Matt says. I nod gratefully. "I'm told your parents are waiting for you at the hospital."

"Really?! They're not hurt?" I ask.

"Safe and sound. Your brother is fine, too."

I think of them sitting there waiting for my arrival and my heart leaps. I can't wait to see them.

"Got a little crazy while I was gone, did you?" Matt chuckles as he straps me into the stretcher.

"Ha. A piece of metal tried to take me out," I tell him.

"We'll all breathe a little easier once you guys are all out of here," Matt says. "This building is pretty beat up, too."

People start stepping forward to wish me well. The sales women, Olivia, and Nancy each give me a hug.

"You helped keep us safe," Nancy says. "And you saved George's life."

I blush. "I don't know about that."

Brandon takes his turn. "You sure did. You gotta stop selling yourself short, Zach. You're stronger than you think. I heard that from someone once. It turned out it was great advice." He winks at me.

I look around for Peter and Mildred. Mildred is being tended to by another paramedic. Peter watches over her lovingly.

Cooper pats me on the chest. "We'll try to get to the hospital as soon as we can. My parents took a grid road around the city." Oh good. Cooper's parents are safe, too.

"Okay, thanks, Coop."

He steps out of the way so that Samara can get closer. She squeezes my hand again.

"I'm so glad you're still here," I tell her. "Are you okay?"

"Of course, I am. I'm not the one lying on a stretcher."

"I don't want anything to happen to you," I say. The paramedics whistle, teasing me for being lovey-dovey.

"It's your turn for a helicopter ride," Matt says. "We've got to get going."

"How will I see you?" My voice cracks as I study Samara. I don't want to leave without her.

"I'll bring her with me," Cooper says. He looks back and forth between the two of us.

"Will you? That would be great. Thanks, Cooper!" Samara says. I nod at him gratefully. She gives me one last squeeze before letting go of my hand.

Matt tightens the five-point harness around my chest. "Say goodbye!"

I hear "Bye, Zach!" in several voices as Matt wheels me toward the food court doors. The sun warms my face. I squint from the sudden light and the swift wind generated by the helicopter blades. After the brutality of the storm, it's actually shaping up to be a beautiful day.

The paramedics lift my stretcher into the helicopter and the door clicks behind us.

– – – –

As I'm being wheeled into the emergency room, I hear my mom's voice. "Zach!!" She runs toward me and cups my cheeks in her hands, leaning over me.

Part of me wants to throw my arms around her because I'm so happy to see her, but I decide to play it cool. "It's okay, Mom. I'm fine."

"This doesn't look fine."

"No, really. I'm okay." My dad and Marshall step forward from behind my mom. They look so relieved to see me that my eyes immediately pool with tears.

They follow as Matt wheels me toward a room. Nurses immediately join us.

"Zach!" I hear. I try to turn my head but it's hard to do with this plastic collar around my neck. A wheelchair comes into view. It's Chris. His face is stitched up and he's got a lot of scratches, but he's grinning from ear to ear. Then I see he's holding a baby, bundled up tightly in blankets.

"It's a girl!" he yells. I give him a thumbs-up. I don't know how he got here, but I'm sure happy he did. Chris is wheeled away.

Again, my eyelids start to feel heavy. The emergency room is loud, bright, and chaotic, but it can't compete with the exhaustion I feel. I try to stay awake but my eyes close and make the decision for me.

- - - -

When I open my eyes, I'm greeted by Cooper and his parents.

Cooper steps in and holds out his hand. We do our special handshake and he pats my shoulder.

"Thanks," I say. "Where's Samara?" I hear two women's voices laughing. My mom is obviously having a good time visiting with someone. Samara steps out from behind my dad and Marshall. She was the one laughing with my mom.

She's smiling broadly.

"Are you okay?" I ask again.

"Why do you keep asking if I'm okay?" Samara laughs. "I'm perfectly fine."

"Did the doctors check your cuts?"

Samara waves me off as though the cuts on her legs are nothing.

"Look. I'm not some Princess Peach you need to rescue," she says. "I can take care of myself just fine." Her face remains serious. "And if you're going to typecast me as anyone, at least make it better than Peach. I think I'm far more badass than that."

"Lara Croft?" I suggest.

"Better be the newer version. Not the half-naked, big-boobed, unrealistic-body-proportions one." Samara smiles. "You're getting closer."

"Good, because I don't want to be Mario," I say with a smile. A short, stout, pudgy plumber with a giant black moustache. Not exactly my idea of a hot date.

"You're my Link," Samara decides.

I like that. Link is one of the most beloved characters in video game history; he's from the *Legend of Zelda*. Link and Princess Zelda are young adults who continually face the challenges of both adulthood and having to save the world before they're ready for it. I think it sums up nicely what we've just been through.

Link's a brave hero who is both capable and humble. He lives to defeat bad guys and evil forces. But he's also the strong, silent type. Link doesn't say much.

"But I can talk, right?" I ask.

"Yes." Samara smiles.

"What about kiss?"

"Definitely!" Samara giggles. She places her hands on my shoulders and draws her face close to mine. Our noses brush together. I feel her warm breath on my lips. My entire body tingles with her so close to me. My dad clears his throat, and I'm hit with the image of Toad rushing into the room to tell me that my princess is in another castle.

A hero has to do everything he can until his last breath. He must do what he's been sent to do and complete his mission.

Even though the room is filled with people, I can't imagine a better moment. It's the moment I've been hoping for, waiting for … and it's as incredible as I imagined it would be. Samara's lips touch mine — so gently and softly I press for more. Her kiss makes me dizzy with joy. No matter how many times I've imagined being the hero in the gaming world, there's one thing I can say: reality is *always* better. I wrap my arms around her as best I can and pull her closer.

And that is how the gamer gets the girl.

ACKS

[Acknowledgements]

I'd like to send a huge thank you to the staff at Dundurn Press who work tirelessly for the love of all things reading. Your passion for your work is evident in the books you craft. Thank you to Kirk Howard, Sheila Douglas, Kathryn Lane, Kathryn Bassett, Heather McLeod, Tabassum Siddiqui, Synora Van Drine, Michelle Melski, Kendra Martin, Laura Boyle, and the rest of the Dundurn Press team. Laura, this cover is boss!

A special thanks to Jess Shulman for her editing expertise; I love working with you, Jess! You are incredible at what you do. I am fortunate to have had two of my books placed in your more-than-capable hands.

A good sounding board is invaluable, and I thank Bev Theriault, Susan McMillan, Danielle Mase, and Maria Deutscher for letting me run ideas by you as the book was crafted and for your coveted advice.

To Matt Hogan, I promised that Paramedic Matt would appear as a character in one of my books someday. Thank you for all you do. Thanks again for your help with *The 11th Hour*.

To Danielle Mase, a special thank you for the numerous pep talks, late-night text messages, and heart-to-hearts we had during the writing of this book. You are a wonderful cheerleader!

To my co-workers at the hospital, especially Marlessa and Lisa, you dazzle me with your talents and your ability to bring joy and comfort to the people we encounter every day. I learn so much from you. You are pure magic!

To Ethan and Kale, for all of the gaming advice and for teaching Mom the ins and outs of what gaming's really about. There's no way I could have written a book like this one without you. To Gracelyn, for always finding ways to carve out the time for me to write somehow.

To Ben — the past couple of years have been the most challenging for us for so many reasons, but there's no one I'd rather do life with. To still love each other after all of these years as fiercely as we do is a blessing and a gift. You'll always have this girl.

To my readers, thank you for taking the time from your busy lives to read my books. Your feedback, support, and reviews mean the world to me. Feel free to get in touch — nothing makes me happier than getting to connect with you!

Book Credits

Project Editor: Jenny McWha

Editorial Assistant: Melissa Kawaguchi

Editor: Jess Shulman

Proofreader: Tara Quigley

Cover Designer: Laura Boyle

Interior Designer: Rudi Garcia

Publicist: Elham Ali

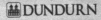